D0871115

THE GUNS OF CALEB JONES

Caleb Jones rode into Desert Bluffs to make peace with his daughter whom he had not seen in twenty years. But Aguilar's raiders, from across the Mexican border, denied him the opportunity, killing her and taking his granddaughters. Then as Caleb rode in to get them back, guns blazing, it seemed that this explosive rescue mission into Mexico was doomed from the start. But Caleb wouldn't accept defeat lying down. When his guns spoke, men listened or died . . .

ALAN C. PORTER

THE GUNS OF CALEB JONES

Complete and Unabridged

LINFORD
Leicester

First published in Great Britain in 2009 by
Robert Hale Limited
London

First Linford Edition
published 2010
by arrangement with
Robert Hale Limited
London

British Library CIP Data

Porter, Alan C., *1959* –
    The guns of Caleb Jones.- -
    (Linford western library)
    1. Western stories.
    2. Large type books.
    I. Title II. Series
    823.9'14–dc22

ISBN 978–1–44480–016–6

Published by
F. A. Thorpe (Publishing)
Anstey, Leicestershire

Set by Words & Graphics Ltd.
Anstey, Leicestershire
Printed and bound in Great Britain by
T. J. International Ltd., Padstow, Cornwall

This book is printed on acid-free paper

To Andrew, Danielle and baby Rianna;
newest addition to the family.

1

The girl shaded her eyes from the sun with a slim hand and squinted through the wind-stirred dust and shimmering heatwaves at a dark, distorted shape that moved in the middle distance across a flat, ochre landscape.

'Rider coming in, Ma,' she called out, her eyes never leaving the approaching shape that was slowly gaining solidity and form as it drew closer. By the time Martha Taplow appeared in the doorway of the cabin, a rifle clutched in her hands, the shape had become a man astride a horse.

Martha levered a shell into the breech of the old Winchester and cradled it across her thin chest.

'Who is it, Ma?' A little girl, no more than eight years old had followed Martha out of the cabin and now stood nervously plucking at her mother's skirt.

'I don't know, Katie. Ellie, take Katie into the cabin and wait inside.'

'But, Ma — '

'No buts, Ellie,' Martha said sharply. 'Do as I say.' Ellie Taplow pouted. 'Yes, Ma.' She brushed a stray lock of golden hair from her pretty face and took hold of Katie's hand. At sixteen years she felt she was old enough to stand at her mother's side and not be sent away, but she knew better than to argue with her mother. 'Come on, Katie.'

Caleb Jones sat hunched in the saddle, dark eyes shaded by the brim of his hat as he stared towards the distant cabin. He raised a bottle to his heavily stubbled lips and took a deep pull of raw whiskey before burying the bottle in his saddle-bag. He felt he needed the help of old John Barleycorn for what lay ahead.

As the rider drew near, the watching woman sensed something familiar about him, but the sun in her eyes clouded her vision.

'That's far enough, mister,' she called

2

and swung the rifle in his direction, digging the stock into her hip. 'State your business.'

'Is that a way to greet your pa, Martha?'

A gasp flew from Martha Taplow's thin lips. She raised her left hand, which had been steadying the rifle, and shaded her eyes. The harsh, unfriendly climate and hard way of life had taken its toll of Martha Taplow, wrinkling the flesh of her thin face, ageing it before its time.

'You!' The word fell from her lips, but there was no warmth of welcome in it nor in the light of hate that flared in her eyes. She dropped her hand back to the rifle and held it on him.

'Mind if'n I step down from the saddle? It's been a long ride an' these old bones could do wi' a stretch,' Caleb Jones called out.

'Twenty years an' you come riding in here as though nothing had happened. Ride on, old man, there's nothing here for you.' Fury coarsened her voice.

The venom in her voice made Caleb flinch.

'I'm sorry you feel like that,' he mumbled.

'How else do you think I'd feel? You deserted Ma an' me an' now, twenty years later, you come riding back an' expect to be made welcome. Ma died waiting for you to come back, she always believed you would. She died five years ago.'

'I heard. I'm sorry,' Caleb said contritely.

'Why have you come here now?' she demanded.

'I did a bad thing leaving you an' your ma. Cain't do anything 'bout that, it's gone, lost for ever, but I figured that mebbe it was time to make things right.'

Tears sparkled in her eyes. 'It's too late for that. I got my own life an' there's no room in it for you.' Her voice shook and trembled as almost forgotten memories filled her mind. Of a big, genial man with gentle hands who used to rock her asleep in his thick, safe arms. Her mother laughing. She swallowed 'Just ride on an' leave us in peace,' she choked.

'Can I at least get some water for my hoss.'

'I got nothing agin the animal. The pump's over there. Water your horse and then go. Get off my land an' don't come back.' As Caleb climbed wearily from the saddle she became aware that she was not alone. Ellie and Katie had crept quietly from the cabin and were staring silently at the big man in the grubby white duster, easing the cricks from his back. Martha became aware of the two girls. She turned her head. 'I told you to stay inside,' she snapped at Ellie.

'Is he really our grandpa?' Ellie asked.

'He's just a drifter passing through. Now get back into the cabin!'

With a pout Ellie returned to the cabin dragging Katie in her wake.

'Fine girls,' Caleb called out as he

worked the handle of the pump, sending water splashing into a wooden bucket.

'And they'll have nothing to do with you. Make sure you're gone when I come out.' With that Martha turned on her heel and marched stiff-backed into the cabin.

Caleb blew out his lips and shook his head as he carried the bucket to where his horse stood and set it down before the animal. As the horse dipped its head Caleb took his hat off to reveal a head of thick, salt-and-pepper hair and ran a sleeve across his sweating forehead. He had known it would be a hard chore to try and win Martha over, but the bitter, naked hatred that showed in her eyes at the sight of him was like a mule kick to the belly, making him glad of the whiskey buffer.

He sighed as he jammed the hat back on his head. He couldn't blame her. He had done a bad thing all those years ago. Why should she forgive him? He was not sure now if he even had the right to ask her.

'Are you really my grandpa, mister?' The tiny voice made him turn and he found himself under the close scrutiny of a pair of big blue eyes.

A smile crossed Caleb's stubble-lined face. He dropped into a crouch before Katie. She clutched a rag doll to her chest.

'Guess I am, button. You must be Katie.'

Katie nodded and held out the doll. 'This is Raggy Annie.'

'Well I'm sure pleased to make your acquaintance, Miss Raggy Annie.'

Katie giggled and drew the doll back to her chest.

'Katie!' Martha appeared at the door of the cabin and raced towards the pair. 'What are you doing out here, child? Get away from him, and get back to the cabin; now!' The final shouted word had Katie running back to the cabin. Martha whirled on Caleb who had now risen to his feet. 'Your horse is watered. Get out of here and outta my life

. . . outta our lives,' she stormed.

A sudden hardness crossed Caleb's face. 'Dammit, girl, like it or not I'm the only pa you've got,' he snapped back. 'The only grandpa the young 'uns have got.'

'And where were you when I needed you? When they needed you? When Ma was dying and when she was finally laid to rest?' She stepped closer, fury making her body shake. 'When my man was shot dead an' I was left alone to raise Ellie an' Katie? We needed you then but we sure don't need no worn-out, whiskey-smelling soak now. Just get off my land an' outta our lives!'

'Guess you don't,' he replied softly. 'Obliged for the water, ma'am.' He swung himself back into the saddle. 'I'll be staying in town a coupla days if'n you feel like talking.' With that he jerked the horse's head around and rode off without a backward glance.

Martha watched him go and the anger drained from her body. Tears filled her eyes and rolled down her cheeks.

* * *

'Morning, Walt. Shaping up to be another fine day.'

'Looks that way, Fred,' Sheriff Walt Danvers acknowledged the greeting from the general-store owner before opening the door of his office and stepping over the threshold.

Deputy Luke Jarvis hauled his lean body out of the chair behind the desk.

'How are things, Luke? Quiet night?'

'Only had to haul one drunk in, Sheriff.'

'Quiet night then,' Walt said with a chuckle as he headed for the desk.

'Hey. Any chance a body can get food in this place?' The voice came from behind the closed door at the rear of the office that led into the jail area.

'Sounds like he's awake. Cause any trouble?'

'Shot his gun into the air a coupla

9

times,' Luke replied. 'Figured he was better locked up for the night.'

'Anybody out there hearing me?' the prisoner yelled.

'Got a name for this yahoo?' Walt asked as he reached his desk.

'It's all down in the book, Sheriff. Calls hissel' Jones, Caleb Jones. Is anything wrong, Sheriff?' The question came from the deputy as the sheriff suddenly stopped as though he had walked into an invisible wall.

'Dammit, I thought there was something familiar 'bout the voice.' Walt eyed the anxiously staring deputy. 'Let him out, Luke.'

'You know him, Sheriff?'

'If'n it's who I think it is, then the gent an' I are acquainted from aways back.' Walt picked up the key ring on the desk and tossed it across to his deputy. 'Turn him loose, Luke.'

'Yes, sir.'

Walt was standing at a black, pot-bellied stove, pouring coffee into a chipped enamel mug when Caleb emerged from the cell block.

'So it is you,' Walt said holding out the coffee mug towards Caleb.

Caleb stared at the sheriff. 'Do I know you?' He squinted at the sheriff.

'You should do, Caleb. Tucson, sixty-eight. Deputy Walt Danvers.'

Caleb stared at Walt for a long minute, then the light of recognition flooded into his eyes. He took the mug being proffered and raised it to his lips. He took a mouthful of the hot coffee without flinching. He eyed the badge pinned on the other's chest.

'So you made sheriff,' Caleb observed.

'Only because o' you. Sit down, Caleb. What the hell happened to you?'

'Life, I guess,' Caleb said. He flopped into a seat before the desk while Walt dropped into the seat behind. 'Got to enjoy it too much.' A sad smile tugged at Caleb's lips.

'What brings you to Desert Bluffs, Caleb?'

Caleb sipped his coffee. 'Family business, Walt. Trying to set things straight afore it's too late, although it may already be too late.' Caleb did not elaborate and Walt did not push.

'Plan on staying long?'

'Probably not. Didn't do too well at the family business yesterday.' Caleb drained his cup. 'I needed that.' He climbed to his feet. 'Need to get mysel' cleaned up afore I try agin.'

'Might be an idea,' Walt agreed, then: 'You wouldn't be pulling the old Charley Pearson trick, would you, Caleb?'

A smile appeared on Caleb's face. 'Sure beats paying for a hotel for the night. Thanks for your hospitality, Walt, an' you too, Deputy. Can I have my gunbelt back?'

'Luke, give the man back his property, and, Caleb ... Charley Pearson only works once. Next time it'll be a ten-dollar fine.'

Caleb waved a hand as the deputy handed him his gunbelt.

'I'll remember, Walt.' Draping the gunbelt over his shoulder Caleb stamped

12

out of the office.

Luke looked across at Walt. 'Who is he, Sheriff? Did you know him from somewhere?'

Walt eyed his deputy. 'Caleb Jones was a legend in his time. He was one of the best lawmen an' the most feared by lawbreakers. A real, living town-tamer an' I was his deputy in Tucson for near on five years,' came the surprising revelation.

'Hell, Sheriff, is that right?' Luke said.

'You'd better believe it, Luke. Caleb used to wear a two-gun rig fastened wi' a silver horse's-head buckle an' he could fast draw wi' either hand, or, if needs be, both hands, an' could shoot in two different directions at the same time. Ain't many could do that. He was one hell of a man.'

'What happened to him then, Sheriff?'

'Drink happened,' Walt shook his head. 'Drink, fame an' women. He left his wife, an' in the end the drink cost him his job an' he vanished. This is the first time I've seen him in twenty years.'

Luke frowned. 'Who's this Charley Pearson, Sheriff?'

Walt smiled. 'He was a drifter, rolled into Tuscon from time to time an' spent his money on drink. When the money ran out he'd start firing his gun an' we'd have him hauled off to spend the night in jail.' The sheriff's smile broadened. 'Found out later he did the same thing in every town he went to.'

Luke's frown deepened. 'Why would he do that?'

''Cause it got him a bed for the night an' a breakfast in the morning an' it didn't cost him a cent.' Walt chuckled at the memory as he reached for his coffee.

*　*　*

Caleb lurched down the sidewalk, the previous night's drink still working on his body, the early-morning sun making him squint. He grabbed at the hitch rail outside the general store and held on, sucking air, waiting for the moment to pass. A wagon approached followed by a knot of people. He detected a buzz of excitement.

'What's happening,' he called out to a rider accompanying the wagon as it came abreast. In the flatbed of the wagon a yellow slicker covered a still form.

'Raiders hit the Taplow spread last night. Killed Martha Taplow an' took her daughters,' the rider called out as he passed.

2

The news hit Caleb like a physical blow. His legs sagged and he gripped the rail with knuckle-whitened hands to stop himself falling. He stared open-mouthed at the back of the rider, heart pounding fit to burst before launching himself off the sidewalk and running after the wagon, booted feet pounding the rutted, hard-packed earth of Main Street, his own drink-induced troubles forgotten. He caught up with it as it came level with the sheriff's office and the driver hauled back on the reins.

Caleb pushed roughly through the knot of people to get to the flatbed wagon. A yellow slicker had been draped over the body, Caleb reached over the side and gently peeled it back to reveal the white, staring-eyed face of his daughter, Martha Taplow.

'What the hell do you think you're

doing, mister?' the wagon driver shouted. 'This ain't no peepshow!' At that moment Walt, closely followed by Luke, emerged from the office.

'What in tarnation is going on here, Ben?' Walt called up to the driver.

'Raiders hit, Sheriff. Taplow woman's dead an' her girls gone, an' this damn fool,' he jerked a thumb at Caleb, 'he's after getting a look at the body.'

'What's going on, Caleb?' Walt asked roughly, planting himself squarely before the stricken man, who had replaced the slicker and stepped back numbly from the wagon.

'Martha Taplow was my daughter,' Caleb mumbled. 'She was the reason I came here.'

Walt's mouth fell open.

'Daughter! Jesus, Caleb. I'm sorry, I didn't know.' Walt took a hold of Caleb's arm. 'Let's go in the office. Ben, get the body over to the undertaker,' Walt called up to the driver, 'an' get Doc Robson to examine it.' Walt eyed Caleb. 'Need to get a

17

proper certificate o' death. You know the way it is.'

Caleb nodded dumbly and Walt wasn't sure if the man had taken it in or what. He led Caleb into the office and sat him in the chair that he had occupied earlier. Walt filled a couple of mugs with coffee from the stove.

'Bad business, Caleb. Sounds like Aguilar's Raiders have struck agin.' Walt shook his head.

'Came here to make my peace wi' her,' Caleb said as though he had not heard the sheriff's words. He sat hunched in the chair, gripping the coffee mug with both hands. 'First meeting didn't go too well. She was angry, Walt, an' who could blame her? Figured to give her a day or two to cool down an' try agin. Ain't gonna be able to now.' Caleb took a sip of his coffee and suddenly the slackness of his face tightened. Anger filled his eyes and in a spasm of fury he threw the mug across the room. 'Dammit to hell, Walt!' he shouted. 'I ain't never gonna get the chance to make my peace wi' her now.' Caleb clambered to his feet, spun on his heel and headed for the door without another word.

'Caleb, where are you going?' Walt called after him.

'I'll be back,' Caleb replied as he left the office.

Walt shook his head sadly in the wake of the man's departure, then busied himself with office work.

★　★　★

More than an hour had passed since Caleb's departure. Doc Robson had delivered his report, which did not make pretty reading, and had signed a certificate of death on Martha Taplow. The undertaker had not long departed, wanting to know about arrangements for the burial, for burials were quick affairs in this part of Arizona mainly on account of the heat. And to top it all no one had seen Caleb since he had left the office.

Luke came into the office after doing his rounds and headed for the coffee pot on the stove.

'Seen or heard anything o' Caleb?'

'Nary hide nor hair, Sheriff. Collected his horse from the livery stable an' ain't no one seen him since.' Luke filled a mug with coffee and turned to face the seated sheriff as the outer door opened and a shadow stretched itself across the wooden floor. Luke had the mug halfway to his lips as his eyes flickered on to the owner of the shadow and he froze on the spot. Walt's eyes popped and his jaw slackened, falling open.

'Caleb?' Walt managed to splutter out.

Caleb Jones moved towards the seated sheriff, but it was not the hunched, dirty, whiskey-smelling Caleb Jones who had graced the town's jail the previous night. The man walking towards him stood tall and steely-eyed, a black, low-crowned hat on his head. A long bath and a whole pot of coffee

20

followed by a shave had started the transformation, The dark three-piece suit, instead of the dusty, worn and frayed range clothes, continued the change and the double holster with a pair of matched, pearl-handled, single-action Colt Peacemakers, buckled with a silver horse's head, completed the transformation.

'Tell me 'bout the raiders you mentioned when you heard my girl had been killed, Walt.' Caleb sat himself down in the chair before the desk and stared frostily at Walt.

Walt leaned back slowly in his chair and ran a hand across his lips.

'You kept the guns an' what you used to call your 'business suit' all these years, Caleb?'

'Been a time since I've worn either. Never thought I'd ever wear 'em agin 'cept at my own funeral. So, 'bout these raiders?'

'Aguilar's Raiders. They come across the border from Mexico, led by one Rafael Aguilar, taking women an' young girls. They auction 'em off to whoever's willing to buy. Mexican, Indian, American even.'

'How come they get away with this?' Caleb demanded.

'Because the desert's a big place an' once across the border into Mexico we can't touch them. The Mexican authorities are not interested.'

'So they ride in, take our women an' no one goes after them?'

'Send any sort of force across the border into Mexico an' you'll have a war on your hands. Our government's hands are tied an' the Mex authorities know it. The only chance we have is to catch Aguilar an' his men on our side o' the border an' so far it ain't happened. The army has a patrol riding the border, but Aguilar's too damn clever for 'em. He struts 'bout Border Town laughing at the blue-bellies.'

'So we do nothin' and' leave our women to mebbe end up in some lousy, Mexican brothel, or worse.' Caleb stared coldly at Walt.

'Like I said, Caleb, ain't nothin' we can do but wait. Aguilar will make a mistake one day an' we'll get him. Until then . . . ' Walt spread his arms.

Caleb stared at him. 'That ain't the way I taught you to uphold the law. If'n a crime's been committed, you go after the lawbreakers, no matter what.'

Walt bridled, stung by the tone in Caleb's voice. 'Now hold on, Caleb. Keeping the law in a town like Tucson is one thing, but out here in the border country keeping the peace is jus' that. You do what you can to keep the peace. One wrong move on our part or their part an' a war wi' Mexico is a real possibility. an' that's something the authorities on either side don' want happening.'

'And to hell wi' the poor folk taken by the raiders.' Caleb rose to his feet. 'It don' sit right wi' me, Walt. It ain't the way I do things.'

'Now hold on, Caleb.' Alarm showed in Walt's voice. 'We cain't have you starting an incident.'

'Got me a funeral to attend to.'

'We gotta talk some more, Caleb,' Walt insisted.

'Sure, Walt. Afore I leave for Border Town.'

'Caleb . . . ' Walt began, but by now Caleb was up and heading for the door.

★   ★   ★

The funeral for Martha Taplow was well attended. She had been a well-liked woman in town and that pleased Caleb. Folk who had heard that Caleb was her father came up to him and paid their respects.

The sun was high in the sky as Martha's coffin was lowered into the ground and the people began drifting away until only Caleb remained at the graveside, staring down into the grave.

'I was never much o' a pa to you, girl, but I aim to be a proper grandpa to your children.' There was a catch in the back of Caleb's throat. 'Tell your ma I was wrong an' that I love her, always did.' He sniffed, tossed a handful of prairie flowers on to the coffin, turned and walked quickly away.

Walt Danvers stood on the edge of the cemetery and fell into step with Caleb.

'If you intend to go to Border Town looking for Aguilar, Caleb, you'll get yourself killed.' Walt said without preamble.

Caleb glanced at Walt. 'You don't waste words do you, Walt. Get straight to the point. I like that.'

'Dammit, Caleb, look at yoursel'. Your town-taming days were thirty years ago. You might look the part wi' your suit an' guns, but are you as fast as you once were?'

'I don't need no wet-nurse, Walt,' Caleb growled.

'I think mebbe you do.' Walt grabbed Caleb's arm and brought him to a halt. 'Let me tell you 'bout Border Town. It's what it says it is. It sits plumb on the border. One half of Main Street is in Mexico the other half is in America. It's full o' the dregs o' both countries and as wild as hell.'

'Aguilar runs the Mex side an' a fella by the name o' Jackson Small does the same for the American side. Ain't no law on either side, 'cepting the law o' the gun. A man would have to be a fool or running from the law to set foot in that town.'

'Guess I'm a fool then,' Caleb said casually.

'A dead fool,' Walt shot back.

Caleb fixed Walt with a steely glare. 'I was robbed o' the chance to get to know my daughter, but I've got two granddaughters that I met for the first time yesterday an' I aim to make sure the first time ain't the last.' With that Caleb turned away and continued his walk into town.

'Mr Jones. I hear you are heading for Border Town. I'd be obliged if'n you'd let me ride with you.'

Caleb was tightening the strap on the saddle roll as the polite voice spoke suddenly from behind him.

'Now why would . . . ?' Caleb swung to face the owner of the voice and the words died in his throat as he faced an Adam's apple jerking nervously behind an open collar. He had to raise his eyes to look into the square-jawed, earnest face topped with rust-coloured hair which peered back at him with green, anxious eyes. Before Caleb stood a giant of a boy, for he could not have been more than nineteen years of age. Clad in black, lace-up boots, a brown jacket and a pair of fawn-coloured pants held up with a pair of red suspenders over a green shirt, he toted a saddle roll over one shoulder and cradled an old, well-loved Winchester rifle to his broad chest.

Caleb swallowed and started again, appraising the youth. 'They sure build 'em big in these parts,' he said and his eyes narrowed. 'Now why would you be wanting to do that, boy?'

'I aim to go after Ellie an' Katie an' avenge the death o' Mrs Taplow, sir.'

Caleb took a step back at the

surprising statement. 'That's my job, boy,' he said gruffly. 'They's my granddaughters them hellions took, an' my daughter they used an' murdered. Just who are you, boy, an' why is it your business?'

'My name's Nathan Burgess, sir, an' I've been walking out wi' Miss Ellie since the spring.'

Caleb's scowl deepened. 'I hope you ain't been dallying wi' my grandaughter's affections, boy,' Caleb roared.

Nathan's face reddened. 'I have not, sir, an' I'll fight anyone who says different,' he cut back belligerently. 'Miss Ellie is the kindest, most gentle, sweetest girl an' we hoped to get married in the fall. Mrs Taplow looked upon me wi' some favour.' It was Nathan's turn to glare now and there was fighting fire in his green eyes.

'I reckon you would,' Caleb murmured, taking in the big hands that clutched the Winchester. 'Happen Mrs Taplow favoured you, boy, but I travel alone. I don't got no time to nursemaid no greenhorn.'

'I can look after mysel', sir. With or without you I'm heading for Border Town.'

'Dammit, boy, you'll get yoursel' killed for sure, an' what use'll you be to my Ellie, dead?'

Nathan fixed Caleb with a level stare. 'What use would I be to her if'n I stayed here an' did nothing?'

Caleb stared long and hard at the young man, as for once in his life he could find no answer to the question.

'Do your folks know of your hare-brained intention?' he said at last.

'My pa, for my ma died when I was a young'un, he said that if'n a woman was worth fighting for, then you fight.'

'Can you kill a man?'

'I don't know, sir, never had cause to kill anyone,' came the truthful reply.

'The place we're headed, the folks there don' need no cause to kill, they just do it for fun.'

'I understand that, sir.'

Caleb sniffed. 'Can you use a gun?'

'Tolerable, sir. Ain't no fancy draw

wi' a pistol, fingers too big, but . . . '
Nathan looked up and Caleb followed
his gaze. High overhead a trio of crows
circled lazily. Nathan levered a shell
into the breech of the Winchester,
raised it and squeezed off three shots in
rapid succession. The circling birds
exploded in blood and feathers. 'Wi' a
rifle I've yet to be beaten in the annual
county shoot-out.'

Caleb was impressed at the boy's effort-
less ease in dispatching the moving targets.
He nodded his head approvingly.

'What in tarnation's going on here,
Caleb?' Walt came charging up with his
deputy in tow.

'Jus' a little pest control, Walt,' Caleb
returned brightly.

★ ★ ★

As night fell across the desert Caleb
poured a second mug of coffee from a
pot set on a small, flickering fire. The
flames picked out his features with a
mixture of amber light and shadows.

On the other side of the small fire Nathan lay stretched out on a blanket, staring up at the star-filled sky using a saddle-bag as a pillow. The two had left Desert Bluffs in the early afternoon, Caleb anxious to cut as many miles as possible before dark off the seventy-mile journey to Border Town.

'Figure we'll hit Border Town by noon tomorrow,' he had said as he kindled the brushwood fire. Their campsite for the night was amid a cluster of rocks rising from the sand. He had surmised it was probably the remains of something larger, which the wind-blown sand had eroded to what now remained.

Caleb drained his mug as off in the distance came the lonely wail of a coyote. Nathan stirred. He rolled on to his side, supporting himself on one elbow, looking across at Caleb.

'How do we go 'bout finding Miss Ellie an' Katie when we reach Border Town, Mr Jones?' he asked.

Caleb emptied the coffee dregs from

his mug. 'What were you going to do if'n you were on your own?' Caleb countered.

Nathan pulled a face. 'I'll allow I ain't figured that part out, sir,' he confessed unhappily.

Caleb gave a snort. 'That's the easy part, boy. From what I gathered back in Desert Bluffs, within a few days of the girls being taken, this Aguilar *hombre* holds an auction, selling them off to the highest bidder. What we gotta do is get ourselves invited to this here auction. After that it gets a tad more difficult. I heard that a wagon carrying a family o' five by the name o' Baker, travelling outta California, was hit the same night as my girls. The ma an' pa were killed an' three daughters taken, so Aguilar's ready to do the sale. 'Pears he don' like to keep 'em too long. An' quit calling me Mr or sir. Seeing as how you are almost family, call me Caleb.'

'Yes, si — Caleb,' Nathan muttered,

his forehead furrowing in a frown. 'How do we get ourselves invited to this auction an' what — '

'Whoa, boy.' Caleb held up a hand. 'You got too many questions floating around in that head o' yourn that I ain't got answers to. One step at a time an' the first step is to get to Border Town. Now get some sleep, figure on leaving at sunup.'

★ ★ ★

Border Town straddled the Arizona/ Mexico border where the Sonoran desert merged with the Desierto De Altar. It was a noisy mixture of both cultures. The wide main street ran east-west. On the north side of the street the sidewalks were backed with brick-and-timber buildings. On the south side the buildings were of white adobe and stucco. Saloons faced cantinas, hash houses faced tortilla kitchens and whorehouses were the same whichever side of the street you were. And while the different cultures faced each other like suspicious women, the mixed populace moved freely together, Mexicans in saloons, Americans in cantinas.

It was bigger than Caleb had previously thought; the sidewalks seethed with people and wagons rattled and creaked up and down the rutted road. Beyond the town a series of ochre-coloured hills punched up through the sand and mesqite, a wrinkling of the land caused by the ridge of the Sierra Madre Mountains that lay to the east.

Caleb and Nathan rode slowly, side by side, down the main street, the Sierra Madres at their backs. The pair hardly drew much more than a cursory glance from those on the sidewalks. Outside Small's Saloon Caleb reined his mount to a halt and slid stiffly from the saddle, kneading his aching back with clenched fists and arching his shoulders back.

'I ain't as young as I used to be,' he

moaned. 'Need a goddam rocking-chair, not a saddle.' Overhead a number of scantily clad women hung over a veranda that fronted the upper level of the clapboard building, calling down lewd comments to the two and shrieking with laughter. Caleb took it in his stride, but Nathan's face was bright red as he followed Caleb through the batwings into the saloon.

Inside it was a big, sprawling place with a long bar against the back wall. To the left was a brightly coloured faro wheel. To the right, where the long bar ended, stairs led up to a railed gallery; next to them was a raised stage on which sat a man in a red-striped vest, playing a piano.

A sea of round tables, their seats occupied, flooded the area before the bar with its brass footrail, and those who either couldn't or didn't want to sit, bellied up to the bar. It was noisy and smoky, voices were loud, the shrieks of the saloon whores even louder.

Caleb gave a nod of satisfaction as he paused in his stride and looked around. 'This is where we start, boy,' he called to Nathan over the noise, and resumed his course to the bar.

3

'Start, sir — Caleb?' Nathan asked a few minutes later after Caleb had secured a bottle and two glasses from the bar and settled at a table crammed into one corner. This he had cleared by unceremoniously dumping a drunk, who had been sprawled across it snoring loudly, on to the floor. The drunk continued to snore oblivious of his positional change.

Caleb poured whiskey into the two glasses and pushed one towards Nathan, who shied away.

'I don't drink, sir,' he said stiffly.

'Under normal circumstances I'd approve, but not here, where drinking an' whoring is a way o' life, an' any that don't are likely to get a bullet in their upright souls. Do I make mysel' plain, boy?'

'Perfectly,' Nathan replied. He lifted

the glass and took a sip, His eyes popped wide open, then closed as his face creased up.

'That's a start,' Caleb said cheerily. He promptly downed his in a single swallow, then refilled his glass. 'What we need,' Caleb continued after wiping his lips, 'is a plan of action. Something to get us noticed.'

Nathan, who had been looking across the crowded bar-room, spoke urgently from the side of his mouth. 'I think we have been noticed.'

Caleb followed his gaze to see a group of five men walking purposefully towards them, the crowd magically melting away to allow them unhindered passage. Four of the men were big, hard-eyed characters protectively surrounding a smaller, slimly built man clad in a well-pressed grey suit with matching vest over a sky-blue shirt, a thin, bootlace tie fastened with a silver Indian-head clasp at the throat. Beneath the brim of a grey hat blue eyes were fastened on the seated pair from a thin, clean-shaven face.

The group paused before the two. The suited man cast an eye on the sleeping drunk on the floor.

'Get rid of him,' he said in a soft voice. Two of the men sprang forward and unceremoniously dragged the unconcious man across the floor by his legs towards the batwings.

He surveyed the two newcomers silently, making Nathan squirm uncomfortably. Caleb returned his gaze without flinching.

'I'm Jackson Small. I own this establishment,' he said.

Caleb came to his feet, face wreathed in a smile and stuck out a hand. 'Hiram P. Chase o' the Virginia Chases, Mr Small. Pleased to make your acquaintance, sir.'

The proffered hand was not taken by Small. Caleb withdrew his and dropped back in his seat.

'You're a long way from home, Mr Chase. What brings you to Border Town?'

'Business, Mr Small. The fame o' your town is well known, even in the

Blue Ridge Mountains, yes, sir.' Caleb nodded. 'Fine place you have here.'

'That's the way we like to keep it, Mr Chase. And knowing who comes into my saloon helps keep it that way.'

'Cain't be too careful,' Caleb agreed.

'That's why I'm curious to know what sort o' business a man from the Blue Ridge Mountains expects to do in Border Town?'

Caleb smiled. 'It's like this, Mr Small. Got me an establishment like this on the Ridge — well, it ain't as grand as this, but it's a place where a man can gamble, drink an' dally wi' the ladies. Ain't that right, Ned?' He addressed a bemused Nathan who had no chance to answer as Caleb galloped on: 'Ned here's my nephew, learning the business, so to speak. Promised my sister, his dear mother, that I'd look after him after his pa died.' Caleb leaned forward conspiratorially and lowered his voice a mite. 'He ain't too bright, but he's willing to learn. Ain't that right, Ned?' Caleb eyed Nathan,

40

this time waiting for an answer. In fact Nathan felt himself under close scrutiny from all eyes.

'Y-yes, sir, U-Uncle,' he stammered.

Caleb beamed. 'He's a good boy. Don' say much, but he listens.' Caleb nodded, then the smile faded from his face as he looked up at Jackson Small. 'Fact is, Mr Small, I need some new ladies, ladies to fire up the blood o' them mountain boys an' I heard tell that Border Town is the place to come to freshen up my stock, so to speak. Heard rumours that if'n a man had the money, then there ain't nothin' he cain't buy here. Is that right, Mr Small, or have I had a wasted journey?'

'Mebbe, mebbe not,' Small said casually. 'Enough money can buy anything.'

'I got the money, Mr Small. Jus' need a push in the right direction. Heard it said when we passed through Desert Bluffs that special auctions selling women happen around here an' there could be one coming up real soon.

That's one me an' Ned would surely like to attend.'

'You seem to have heard a lot, Mr Chase.'

'In our business you get to hear a lot,' Caleb agreed expansively. 'Ain't that right, Ned?'

'Sure is, U-Uncle,' Nathan supplied, playing along with Caleb's ruse. All through Caleb's account the faces of the men accompanying Jackson Small had remained mean and hard. They were still the same now and it made him feel nervous.

'And what do you call your little establishment?'

Caleb beamed again. 'The Chase Palace,' he replied without hesitation. 'Thought o' that name mysel',' he added proudly.

'Very good, Mr Chase,' Small murmured. 'Where are you staying in Border Town?'

'Jus' rode in. Ain't had time to find no hotel yet.'

'Try Brown's, down the street apiece.'

With that Small turned his back on the two.

'What 'bout my little problem, Mr Small. Can you help me there?' Caleb called after him.

Jackson Small paused and turned back to Caleb. 'You're on the wrong side o' town, Mr Chase. Paco's is the place for you. If Paco likes you he may be able to give the answer you want to hear.'

'An' if'n he don't?'

'Someone will probably find your bodies out in the desert,' Small said ominously and Nathan noticed that the men with Small were smiling for the first time.

* * *

Paco's cantina was tiny compared with Small's place. Tiny and dingy. There were a dozen tables scattered about, mostly around the walls, but it seemed that the clientele of Paco's preferred to crowd the bar. Inside, the stale air was

43

heavy with the smell of chilli and cheap cigars. The sounds that issued from within were much the same as in any saloon, be it Mexican or American. Loud voices, female shrieks, but all sounds ceased the moment the two walked in.

'Howdy *amigos*,' Caleb called out breezily and found himself under the scrutiny of a lot of hostile eyes. 'Mighty hot day out there,' Caleb continued, seemingly oblivious to the sudden, charged atmosphere their presence had generated.

The pair had come to a halt as the crowd along the bar refused to part for them.

'Got any more bright ideas, Uncle?' Nathan whispered in Caleb's ear.

'I'm working on it,' Caleb returned quietly. It was then that a man appeared from the right, pushing his way through the drinkers until he stood, smiling, before the two newcomers. He was a small, colourfully attired Mexican with dark, glistening black hair which was tied in a ponytail.

'*Buenos dias, señores.* Can I be of assistance?'

'Sure could do wi' a tequila or three to lay the dust. Are you Paco?'

'*Sí, señor.* If you would care to be seated. I will have tequila brought for you and your *compadre.*'

'Now that's real neighbourly. Ain't that neighbourly, Ned? Ned here's my nephew an' I'm Hiram P. Chase. Pleased to meet you, sir.' He stuck out a hand and this time Paco took it and they shook. That seemed to be the signal for the patrons of Paco's to return to normal and the hum of voices, girly giggles and shrieks brought life to the silence.

Paco clicked his fingers at the bar, then ushered the two to a table. A few seconds later a barman appeared. He placed a bottle of tequila on the table before Caleb and three glasses, then was gone.

'What brings you to Paco's, *señor*?' Paco asked, sitting on a chair and

45

pouring tequila into the glasses.

'Reckon you an' me could do some business, *amigo*, if'n what Jackson Small says is true.' Caleb tipped his head back and swallowed the drink in a single gulp. 'Dammit, sir, that's mighty fine tequila. Yes, sir.' He ran a hand across his lips. Nathan was more cautious, taking a sip and pulling a face.

'Your *compadre* does not share your delight, *señor*,' Paco said.

'The boy don't appreciate the finer things life has to offer,' Caleb declared loftily. 'His ma cain't abide strong drink, but I'm hoping to cure him o' that.'

'What is that Señor Small says that makes me of interest to you, *señor*?' Paco asked.

Caleb launched into his story of the Chase Palace and the need for girls to provide for the men who drank and gambled there. Much the same as he had told Jackson Small. 'So that's the way o' it, Paco. I got the money,' Caleb drew a bulging notecase from inside his jacket and thumb-riffled the notes within, 'an' I got the need. Now can you help me?'

Paco licked his lips, eyes hungrily devouring the fat notecase. 'It is dangerous to carry so much money in this town, señor,' he said softly.

'Don' trust banks, amigo; 'sides, it's easier to do business wi' the real thing. don' you worry 'bout me an' my money, we take care o' each other.' Caleb slipped the notecase away. 'Now,' Caleb leaned back in his chair holding the lapels of his jacket, 'can we do business, Paco?'

Paco studied Caleb and Nathan. 'Mebbe there is a man who can assist you in seeking that which you desire,' he said cautiously.

Caleb beamed. 'Sounds like my kinda hombre, Paco. How 'bout you set up a meet wi' him?'

'He is a cautious man, señor. Perhaps five hundred dollars, as you Americanos say, up front, would persuade him of your good intentions?'

Caleb's smile remained fixed. 'I might be a mountain man, but I ain't no greenhorn, *amigo*. I'll pay the man himsel'. That's how we do business in the mountains.'

Paco considered Caleb's offer and shrugged. 'Come back tonight, *señor*, and mebbe I will have an answer for you.'

'Sounds good to me, Paco,' Caleb said agreeably.

'I do not promise anything, *señor*.'

'Then I guess I'll be returning home wi' five thousand dollars still in my pocket.' Caleb rose to his feet. 'C'mon, boy. See you tonight, *amigo*.'

'*Buenos dias*, Señor Chase,' Paco, murmured.

Leaving Paco's they walked their horses down to the livery stable to get them fed and watered before attending to their own needs, which meant a visit to the bathhouse before finding a table in a corner of Annie's Hash House. As they settled down to eat hash browns, steak and gravy, Nathan said softly:

'Was that wise, showing off your money an' all in Paco's?'

'Cain't rightly say it was wise, but necessary. Need to let folks know that I got the money to back up my mouth. Makes 'em hungry to get their hands on it.' Caleb nodded wisely before forking a wedge of steak into his mouth.

'That Paco fella sure looked hungry,' Nathan said.

Caleb smiled. 'The hungrier the better.'

For all its wild reputation, Border Town presented a quiet, sedate face during the afternoon, but Caleb surmised it would be a lot different once darkness fell.

After eating they got a room in Brown's, a seedy, run-down hotel sandwiched between the general store and the livery stable. After wedging a chair under the door handle, for the door had a broken lock, they took the opportunity to grab a little rest and sleep while they were able.

Caleb was not wrong in his assumption about the town, as later he was jerked awake by the sound of gunfire in the street below. The room was in darkness as he joined Nathan at the window. Outside night had fallen. Now was the time for the decent folks of Border Town, for there were a number of legitimate businesses along the street, to retire behind locked doors, leaving the lawless to take over the town.

Down below a bunch of riders were hollering and shooting off their pistols.

Caleb turned away from the window and set a kerosene lamp to burn low before buckling on his gunbelt and reaching for his hat.

'Time to roll, boy. Let's see what this town's made of.'

Lamps burned on buildings on both sides of the street. Some flickered and jumped on almost spent wicks, throwing dancing shadows over the baked, rutted earth. The biggest concentration of light came from Jackson Small's saloon. By contrast the Mexican side of the street was gloomier, light spilling from the adobe-walled buildings was subdued. Whores had appeared on both sides of the street, their shrill cries and promises of a night to remember, punctuated by bouts of laughter, filling the air.

Paco's was full as the two entered. Eye-stinging, acrid cigar smoke lay like a fog bank about the two ceiling-hung kerosene lamps, cutting the light to a dirty, lambent, yellow glow. Caleb pushed his way to the bar, shouldering those in his way aside and receiving hostile glares.

'Hey, *amigo*, Paco 'bout?' he called to a moustachioed barman. The barman stared with a vacuous look. 'Paco,' Caleb called again over the noise.

'Tequila?' the barman replied in a gutteral tone.

Caleb pulled a face. '*Dónde esta Paco?*' he tried again in his limited Spanish, asking: 'Where is Paco?'

'*Señor?*'

Caleb blew out his cheeks. 'Dammit!' he cried, pulled a gun and fired three shots in quick succession at the ceiling. The noise was thunderous and people scattered in alarm as chunks of the ceiling rained down, leaving a fist-sized hole in the ceiling.

'Hell, that's better. Fresh air,' cried Caleb, squinting up and then around. The cantina had suddenly gone quiet.

There was movement in the press of people and Paco appeared, pushing his way through until he stood before Caleb.

'Señor Chase.'

'Hi there, Paco. Having a bit o' trouble making mysel' understood.'

Paco stared at the hole in the ceiling. 'You seem to have solved that problem, señor,' he observed, returning his gaze to Caleb.

'Sorry, Paco. Jus' anxious to see if'n we have a deal.'

Paco swept his eyes around the sea of faces and barked out some rapid Spanish that Caleb could not understand. Instantly the crowd broke up and continued as before.

'There is one here who wishes to meet you, *señor*.'

'Then point him out, Paco, an' let's get this show on the road.'

'He is over there. Come.' Without further preamble Paco turned and pushed his way through the crowd with Caleb hot on his heels. Nathan prepared to follow but his path was blocked by two, grim-faced, poncho-clad Mexicans.

'Hey, what's going on?' Caleb said, turning back as Nathan called after him in alarm.

'I do business with you, *señor*, not with a boy.' Caleb whirled around at the voice and found himself facing a handsome, dark-haired Mexican, seated at a small table. On either side of the seated man stood two big, glowering Mexicans, arms folded across their chests as they cradled Winchester rifles to their chests.

Caleb came to a halt and thrust thumbs behind the buckle of his gunbelt, giving the handsome man an insolent stare.

'Raphael Aguilar?'

The man inclined his head before regarding Caleb with button-black eyes.

'Five hundred American dollars. That is the price. For that you will be taken to a place in the hills where you can bid for what you seek.'

'Now what makes you think I'm gonna part up wi' five hundred dollars to a man I don' know? How do I know you an' Paco ain't in this together? I give you the money an' that's the last I see o' you an' it.'

The Mexican eyed him. 'You don't, señor, but if you do not our business ends here and you can return to your mountains with nothing to show but saddle sores.'

The two stared at each other. Then a smile spread across Caleb's face. 'Reckon you've got me over a barrel there, señor.' He drew out his notecase and pulled out some bills, tossing them on the table before the man. 'Guess a little trust is in order. So what happens now?'

The man did not touch the money.

'A mile south of town. There lie the ruins of an old mission on a hill. Be there at dawn tomorrow. A guide will be waiting to take you the rest of the way. *Adios*, Señor Chase.'

At those words the two rifle-toting guards stepped forward and stood shoulder to shoulder before Caleb, blocking out the seated man.

'Yeah, *adios, amigo*,' Caleb called out. 'Nice doing business with you.'

By the time Caleb reached Nathan and looked back the man and his two guards had melted away, as had the guards who had blocked Nathan's way.

'That seemed easy enough,' Nathan said, relieved.

'Mebbe too easy,' Caleb murmured thoughtfully. 'Let's get out of here, boy. We'uns have got an early start in the morning.'

★　★　★

The early-morning light softened the hills beyond Border Town, merging

55

ochres and reds into a dull brown. At the moment a chill came off the desert causing the two riders to hug their coats across their chests. But soon the sun would rise above the distant Sierra Nevadas to the east and the morning chill would turn to a shimmering heat.

The remains of the mission stood on top of a low hill. A few broken walls were dominated by the central bell-chamber, rising against the dark blue of the sky. The bell had long since disappeared and only half the bell-chamber remained intact.

The trail up to the mission ran through clumps of spiky-leafed agarves and fat barrel cactus.

'S'posing this guide don't turn up?' Nathan asked.

'Son, I do declare, you worry too much,' Caleb replied as they came within the shadows of the broken walls, 'but you can stop your worrying. Here he comes.'

As they were speaking a rider appeared through an archway beneath the broken bell-chamber. A colourful poncho was wrapped about his shouders. He reined his mount to a halt and stared at the two from beneath a white sombrero.

'Are you waiting for us, *amigo*?' Caleb called out, a cautious hand resting on the butt of a pistol.

'Come!' the rider said and with no further greeting turned his horse back through the archway into what had once been the main body of the mission but was now a mass of weeds and rubble beneath the open sky. Beyond the ruins of the mission the land wrinkled and creased in a series of folds that spread away like a carelessly discarded blanket.

They followed the rider deep into the steep foothills that abutted the Sierra Nevadas. The trail wound up through scrub oak and juniper that clung tenaciously to the edge of a canyon, which fell to a foaming river far below.

The trail turned inland for a while

before curving back to follow the snaking path of the canyon.

'Hey, *amigo*. How much further we gotta go?' Caleb called out, but the rider took no notice. Caleb eyed Nathan. 'Talkative type, ain't he?'

They rounded a bend and alarm flashed in Caleb's eyes. The guide had disappeared.

'Where in tarnation did he go?' Caleb eyed Nathan in disbelief.

'*Buenos dias*, Señor Chase.' Aguilar appeared ahead on the trail. His bodyguards accompanied him and behind them rode a further six riders who filtered forward as the trail widened, forming a horseshoe with Caleb and Nathan at the open end.

Caleb flashed Nathan a worried glance, but the face he turned to the Mexican was affable and unworried.

'Good day, *señor*. I see you are an honourable man. Could'a kept the five hundred an' disappeared.'

'Which is more than can be said of you, *señor* . . . ' the man paused, peering intently at Caleb. ' . . . Jones, Señor Caleb Jones.' He smiled, then the smile dropped and his face darkened. 'Kill them both!' he hissed.

4

Caleb barely had time to register the shock at hearing his name spoken. That would come later, if there was a later!

Instinctive reaction made him drive the heels of his boots hard into the flanks of his horse, while at the same time he hauled back on the reins. With a whinny of pain, ears laid back, the animal rose up on its hind legs, pawing the air with its front legs. Momentarily the horse became a shield as the Mexicans raised their weapons.

'Get the hell outta here, boy. Ride!' he bellowed as his horse settled back on all four legs. This time Caleb's hands were full. The rearing horse had made the Mexicans hesitate until they had a clear shot at the Americano. It was a hesitation that would cost them dearly.

The guns of Caleb Jones roared in unison as he fired, thumbed back the hammers and fired again in a rapid, fluid movement. For a moment confusion came to Caleb's aid. Aguilar's men, taken by surprise at Caleb's unexpected reaction, tried to get out of the line of fire. Horses crashed into horses, unseating their riders, the Mexicans yelling and howling in panic. A few fired back from the saddles of spooked horses, their aim wild.

Nathan fought to control his own animal as bullets buzzed around him like angry hornets. Then, just when he had his mount under control a bullet hit the animal in the neck. It gave a piteous cry and shied to one side, snapping its head around towards the source of the pain, eyes bulging, ears laid back. Nathan, in the act of pulling his saddle pistol, dropped it as the animal bucked and side-stepped and he had to grab the pommel to save himself from being thrown.

His mount turned in a complete circle. More bullets hit it and Nathan felt a flash of red-hot pain as a bullet grazed his upper left arm, but he had little time to consider his own hurts as his mortally wounded animal, its legs giving out from under him, fell sideways into a wall of juniper. Branches snapped and gave way to thin air as the now dead animal fell through the juniper thicket into the open space of the canyon beyond.

Nathan, in trying to throw himself from the falling animal, managed to get his right foot free of the stirrup but in his panic his left foot became trapped. With a yell of fear he was dragged into the void as the horse plummeted towards the silver band of the river which twisted and turned as it boiled over the rocks 500 feet below.

The gun battle was short-lived but, by the time it was over, five of Aguilar's men lay dead and four more were injured. Caleb himself, guns empty, could do nothing now but rise, his face set, from the sparse cover he had dived into. He had heard Nathan's terrified cry and caught a glimpse of the young man being dragged to his death into the canyon. But he had little time to reflect on the other's demise as the remainder of Aguilar's men gathered, sullen-faced, around him. He raised his hands.

'Well, what are you waiting for. Get on wi' it, you varmints!' he snapped. He was not sad for himself. He had led a life of dodging bullets and cheating death, so it was inevitable that one day death would catch up to him. That day, it seemed, had finally come!

No, his sorrow lay in the death of Nathan and more so for the terrible fate that awaited his granddaughters whom he was helpless to do anything about.

There was movement from the rear of the group and Aguilar, sandwiched between his two beefy bodyguards, appeared before him.

'I must congratulate you, Señor Jones. Most impressive.' He regarded Caleb thoughtfully. 'You made a formidable opponent.'

'We aim to please,' Caleb said casually and watched a smile spread across Aguilar's face. 'How long have you known who I was?'

'Since before you rode into Border Town with Nathan Burgess,' came the mocking reply. 'It was amusing to sit back and let you play out your little deception, which, by the way, was very good. Hiram P. Chase was very convincing. I would have believed you had I not known the truth.'

'An' just how did you know the truth? Who told you, Aguilar?' Caleb demanded.

Aguilar laughed. 'So many questions, Señor Jones. Perhaps, before you die, I will tell you so that his name will be the last name you ever hear. My original intention was for you and your companion to die here, on the trail, but I have decided to keep you alive a little longer. I intend to make an example of you to serve as a warning to any others who may harbour thoughts to deceive me.'

'If'n I was you, I'd kill me now.

Could be a real big mistake keeping me alive.'

Aguilar laughed. 'You amuse me, Caleb Jones. Perhaps you will not be so amused tomorrow when you see your granddaughters being sold to the highest bidder.'

'I'm gonna get real pleasure outta killing you, Aguilar,' Caleb intoned darkly, his reply drawing more laughter from Aguilar and also his men.

'I'd like to see that, Señor Jones.'

'Don' worry, Rafael, *amigo*, you'll be the first,' Caleb returned.

'You Americanos. Always ready with the empty threats as a last resort when there is nothing else you can do. To do that, my friend, you will need someone to come to your assistance. Here, in Mexico, there is no one. You are all alone and that is how you will die. Bring him!' With that Aguilar turned on his heel and headed towards his mount, his bodyguards following.

For Caleb there was no mount. His hands were tied behind his back, a rope slipped around his neck and while they rode he was led like a dog in their wake, choking on the dust.

* * *

Twenty feet down from the top of the canyon Nathan clung to a network of brown, dry roots that decorated the sheer rock face like a tattered lace curtain.

He hung there, hardly daring to move. He should have been dead, smashed to pieces on the rocks that littered the river below, but fate had stepped in. At the last minute he had kicked himself loose from the stirrup and, as the horse fell away beneath him, he had reached out blindly, instinctively with his hands expecting to grab nothing but air. His hands smacked against the cliff face and as he felt the tangle of roots scrape against his palms his fingers closed. The weathered roots took his weight, his body swung in and slammed painfully against the rock.

He clung there, right cheek pressed against the rock, heart thrashing wildly in his breast, wondering if this was just a temporary stay of execution.

He had heard the shooting from above followed by the sound of voices; now silence reigned broken only by the soft rumble of the waters far below, and above that by the creaks and snaps that came from the protesting roots that he held in white-knuckled hands. His rifle and a shoulder-bag were still thrown across his back but his hat was gone. Eyes that he had kept closed since slamming into the cliff he now opened and his stomach lurched as he looked along the sheer rock with its web of roots.

Sweat rolled down his face and his mouth was dry. Panic threatened him. He forced himself to stay calm. He tilted his head back and looked up; the top of the cliff with its edging of juniper and oak seemed a long way away. His feet had found purchase in root clumps below him, left leg almost straight, right leg bent at the knee. Gulping down air he gently released his right hand and inched it along, trembling fingers reaching for the thickest of the roots that he could see. He took a grip and cautiously tested it. It made an ominous creaking sound but held. Licking bone-dry lips he began to haul himself up.

It was a slow, painful process for spent, exhausted muscles, but he ignored the pain and willed himself to carry on.

Hand over hand, a few inches at a time, he dragged himself up. His muscles shrieked in silent agony and he could feel his grip loosening in tired hands. Pain, from where the bullet had creased his upper left arm, flared like jabbing needles. He gritted his teeth and continued doggedly on.

He had moved a few precious feet towards the canyon rim when disaster struck. He had latched on to a single, thick section of root. With a brittle, tearing sound the root came away from the rock. Snapping his head up he saw that the root had grown at an angle across the rock face. It was coming from a point some five or six feet to his right. Now, with his weight hanging to it, he felt himself start to swing to the right like a giant pendulum, on a course that dragged him scraping and bumping across the rough face of the rock.

Smaller roots that had grown over the thick root snapped noisily. Skin tore from his knuckles as his hands, folded tightly about the root, rubbed against the rock. The root creaked as stressed fibres within snapped. Praying silently he closed his eyes and clung on for dear life.

★   ★   ★

For Caleb, made to stumble along with the rope around his neck, in the wake of the riders, the journey was a nightmare. His lungs were full of the harsh, acrid trail dust kicked up by the horses' hoofs. He fell once and was dragged, face down, for a number of yards before the rider reluctantly stopped and allowed Caleb to regain his feet.

It took almost an hour before the riders eventually entered a natural, circular amphitheatre ringed with a ridge of high, saw-toothed walls. Here Aguilar and his men dismounted. Caleb, coughing and wheezing, eyes red and streaming with tears, sank thankfully to his knees. Sweat soaked his body and his feet, in boots not made for long-distance walking, were swollen and painful. Aguilar approached the kneeling man.

'Well, Señor Jones, are you still full of that bravado you displayed earlier?' he sneered.

Caleb raised his head. 'Go to hell, you son-of-a-bitch!' he croaked from a dry, tongue-swollen mouth.

Aguilar laughed. 'I think you will get there before me.' His eyes went to the men on either side of Caleb. 'Take him to the cage.'

★ ★ ★

Nathan hauled himself up over the rim of the canyon, crawled forward and then rolled over on his back and lay there, chest heaving, staring up at the sky, hardly daring to believe he was still alive. Somehow the root had held, protestingly taken his weight, as he dragged himself up the rock face until at last he had heaved himself over the edge to safety.

He lay there until his shaking body was still, heaving lungs settled and heart a gentle throb; now only the pain remained, taking over all his joints and invading his muscles with hot knives ... at least, that was what it felt like when he eventually sat up and took stock of his situation.

He still had his rifle and, in his shoulder-bag, two dozen shells and some jerky. He carried no handgun but he had a knife sheathed on his belt. He put rifle and shoulder-bag aside and took his coat off. Blood from the bullet crease stained his left shirt-sleeve. He gingerly peeled his shirt off and

71

examined the wound. It was bloody but not deep. He used his bandanna as a bandage and quickly pulled his shirt and coat back on before staggering to his feet. He had a weapon and food. He squared his shoulders, now all he had to do was find Caleb.

* * *

The cage was exactly what it said it was, a cage made of lodgepole pine timbers each as thick as a man's wrist, bound and held together with stout rope. Caleb was bundled into it and the door fastened with a lock and chain. His hands had been untied and he had been given food and water. Aguilar did not want him passing out for lack of either before the auction. The cage occupied a point near the centre of the circle on a slab of rock in full view of anyone who might be about. To one side were a series of crude cabins and a corral.

The cage was cramped: less than six feet tall and half that wide, making it impossible for him to stand upright. The only choices were to sit with knees jammed under the chin or in a kneeling position. It had been hot when they put him in the cage and Caleb welcomed the night for it came with a breath of coolness that took the fire out of his skin; but later a deep chill settled in. It drove icily into his bones making his body shiver and teeth chatter. Light and warmth spilling from the cabins taunted him. He could hear laughter, the sound of a guitar.

Four kerosene lamps had been lit and placed around the cage so that he could be seen at all times during the night. Regularly, in various stages of drunkenness, men came out to jeer and taunt him. At last, after the long, cheerless night, dawn came, spreading over the eastern rimrock to chase away the cold. With the dawn, more men began to arrive. The smell of coffee and spicy food wafted over him.

As the morning went on the atmosphere in the camp took on a

light-hearted mood as the drink flowed readily to oil up the potential buyers and loosen their wallets. A band appeared and with it a troupe of girls who danced to the frenetic music.

Aguilar appeared as noon approached. He stopped before the cage and eyed Caleb, who had manoeuvered his stiff, cramped limbs into a kneeling position.

'I trust you slept well, Señor Jones,' he taunted.

Caleb stared at the slim, handsome man who had wrought so much misery.

'Damn you, Aguilar,' he rasped from a dry, sore throat, his eyes spitting hate, hands gripping the wooden bars of the cage until the knuckles were white.

'Obviously not,' Aguilar chuckled. 'I will have to send in room service and you can make your complaints to them. But first, something of interest to you. The sale is about to begin. Please feel free to make a bid.' Laughing, Aguilar turned away. At the same time the music and dancing stopped and an air

74

of expectancy settled over the waiting men.

A flatbed wagon had been rolled into place. From one of the cabins a group of frightened, crying girls were herded: a dozen or so. Their hands were tied before them and a rope hobble at their ankles only allowed them enough room to shuffle. The girls were dirty and dishevelled but Caleb recognized Ellie and little Kate huddled together along with three others whom he took to be the Baker girls. The rest were either Mexican or Indian.

A hand squeezed his heart as he gripped the wooden bars. As the girls shuffled closer to the caged man, Ellie saw Caleb and her eyes widened.

'Grandpa!' The word was torn from her trembling lips. Kate turned her head at her sister's cry, stumbled and fell. A jeer went up from the crowd. She was roughly hauled to her feet and given a stinging slap in the face.

A red haze floated before Caleb's tear-filled eyes. The girls were herded up on to the wagon in full view of the waiting men and made to stand along the far edge. A Mexican stood at either end. Aguilar stepped in front of the wagon and raised his hands for quiet.

'In respect of our Americano guest,' he gestured towards Caleb in the cage, 'two golden-haired angels to bring pleasure to any man.' A roar went up as Ellie and Kate were dragged forward to the front edge of the wagon. 'What am I bid for so fair a pair of *señoritas*?'

Voices began to yell when a gunshot brought silence. Caleb craned his head around. A group of six Mexican soldiers clad in midnight-blue tunics with red collars and cuffs, white pants and black stovepipe hats, rode forward. They were led by a huge bull of a man with a scarred face and only one good eye. In his hand he held a pistol.

Men were forced to scatter as the group rode forward. For an instant Caleb thought salvation was at hand, but his hopes came crashing down as the one-eyed man said, 'One thousand

76

dollars, Americano, for the two, plus the other three white girls.' He spat the words out in harsh, guttural tones.

Aguilar stepped forward, a smile on his face.

'Wecome, Colonel Salazar,' he greeted.

'Keep your welcome, Aguilar. Do we have a deal?'

'Unless there are more bids . . . ' Aguilar began.

Salazar leaned forward. 'Do well to remember, Aguilar. I let you and your men ride these hills. That could stop.'

Aguilar forced a smile. 'We have a deal, Colonel,' he agreed.

Salazar tossed Aguilar a roll of money before turning his attention on Caleb.

'What has this man done?'

'He is called Caleb Jones, Colonel, and he killed many Mexicans trying to rescue the fair-haired ones.'

Salazar stared at Caleb with his single eye.

'It is not good to kill Mexicans, Señor Jones.'

'I enjoyed it,' Caleb replied lightly.

77

Salazar grinned displaying broken, yellow teeth. 'As I will enjoy taking care of them, *señor*. Bring the women,' Salazar called out before turning his gaze on Aguilar. 'You will deal appropriately with this man, Aguilar?'

'All is arranged for a most painful death, Colonel,' Aguilar assured him.

The five girls were unceremoniously hauled into the saddles of the soldiers and with Salazar in the lead they rode out of the camp.

It took less than thirty minutes for the remaining girls to be sold and within an hour the camp was empty save for Aguilar and his men. Caleb's saddle and his gunbelt appeared and were unceremoniously dumped on the ground before the cage. Aguilar, now mounted, kneed his horse towards Caleb.

'It is time for us to leave you to your death, Señor Jones. You can reflect on the fate of your girls as you die. Salazar is not a nice man. He runs Fort Diablo, a day's ride to the south. It is a place where soldiers who have difficulty taking orders learn the error of their ways. Salazar is a hard man. When he has finished with the girls he gives them to his men. Their lives will be short and full of pain, as yours is soon to be,' He nodded towards the southern rimrock.

Caleb squinted up. Half a dozen figures stood motionless against the blue sky.

'They are Comancheros,' Aguilar continued. 'Simple traders, but with murderous intent. Your guns and saddle are payment for allowing us to use their land. They will take your boots and clothes before they kill you. I would like to stay and watch, but . . . ' He shrugged, 'I have other business to attend to.'

'You'd better hope they do a good job of killing me, Aguilar. If'n they don't then you are a dead man,' Caleb said.

'They will do a very good job, I can guarantee it. *Adios amigo.*'

Caleb watched as Aguilar and his

men rode away. His eyes returned to the southern rimrock but the figures were gone. Twenty minutes later Caleb heard a sound, turned his head and felt his heart fill his throat. The six Comancheros, riding bareback, had reappeared and slowly, unhurriedly rode towards him.

5

Caleb watched with dull eyes as the six approached. Their olive-skinned faces with high, prominent cheekbones and gaunt, narrow cheeks, a mix of Indian and Mexican, were expressionless. Their assortment of clothing matched their varied parentage: colourful ponchos and shirts, hide vests and red-striped pants; Stetsons and sombreros, one man wore an old, brown dome-topped derby. Hair, lank and black, spilled from beneath their hats, reaching to their shoulders.

No words were spoken as they slid from their saddleless mounts and advanced on Caleb's saddle and gun-belt. The derby-wearer scooped up the gunbelt but it was snatched from his grasp by another who wore a blue cavalry tunic. A few guttural words came from the tunic-wearer, the derby-wearer inclined his head and backed away. The tunic-wearer took off his own gunbelt and strapped on Caleb's double rig. Then he cinched the buckle of his own rig and slipped it over his head and shoulder. They were all heavily armed with pistols, rifles slung across their backs, knives and tomahawks hanging from their waists.

Blue tunic turned bright, dark eyes on Caleb.

'Nice guns, gringo,' he said in a harsh, grating voice. He barked out an order and a man moved forward, picking up the key to the padlock that had been hung around the pommel of the saddle. He undid the padlock and threw the door open, backing away. Blue tunic smiled showing a set of even, white teeth. 'You can come out now, *amigo*,' he invited.

'Mighty kind o' you,' Caleb replied. He knew his situation was hopeless, but if he was to die then he'd die fighting. During their approach he had taken a knife that he kept in his boot and slipped it up the right sleeve of his coat.

Aguilar's men had been sloppy and had not found the knife. He had hoped to use it on the bindings of the cage during the night, but with the constant patrols and the lamps showing any move he made, the opportunity did not present itself. Now all he could hope for was to take at least one of them before they killed him.

He slowly, painfully, shuffled his body to unfold his knees from beneath him until he sat on the floor of the cage, able to thrust his stiff legs out through the open door, grimacing as a cramping pain flared through them, easing himself forward until he sat on the doorway's edge.

Gritting his teeth he dropped from the cage. He meant to launch himself at blue tunic, the knife ready in his hand but his legs gave out under him and he went sprawling, the knife flying from his hand and coming to rest at blue tunic's moccasined feet.

A smile creased blue tunic's face. 'Hey, *amigo*. That was good,' he applauded. He called out something and the other Comancheros laughed. Blue tunic kicked the knife aside and moved forward, driving a foot hard into Caleb's ribs. 'I shall enjoy your death, *amigo*.'

'Why not, I was gonna enjoy yours,' Caleb shot back defiantly as he struggled on to his knees. He sat back on his haunches, looking up at blue tunic's cruel, sardonic face. He had taken out one of Caleb's pistols, found it empty and began to load it from the shell loops on the belt. The other Comancheros had formed up on either side of their leader, silently waiting.

'Mebbe special death for you, *amigo*. Slit open your fat, Americano belly. Put in scorpions, many scorpions. Sew up belly an' let scorpions kill you, from the inside.' He reholstered the now loaded gun and started loading the other. 'Take many hours. Much pain. You scream a lot an' die in *mucho* agony. How do you like that, *amigo*, eh?' He took a kick at Caleb, but Caleb was ready. He caught the foot, twisted it savagely and was rewarded with a sharp, cracking sound. Blue tunic let out a cry of agony, pulled his leg free and fell heavily backwards, gripping his knee.

'Bet that hurt like hell,' Caleb sang out.

Weapons appeared in the hands of the others, bullets were pumped into the breeches.

'No!' blue tunic yelled as he struggled to his feet and stood on one leg. He drew out a knife and regarded Caleb with pain-racked eyes. 'For that I will take out your eyes, *amigo*,' he hissed. 'I will make sure it takes many days for you to die before the vultures strip the flesh from your body.'

'Have I upset you, *amigo*?' Caleb asked innocently.

Rage replaced the pain in blue tunic's eyes. He grabbed a rifle from the nearest man and using it as a support limped gingerly closer to Caleb.

'I should get that seen to, 'breed, or you're gonna have a limp for life.

Reckon your boys ain't gonna take to a leader wi' a limp,' Caleb goaded, hoping for a quick death as blue tunic raised the knife. But at the last moment he stayed his hand. 'Now you will die even slower, *amigo*,' he promised, not knowing that it was the last promise he would ever make. For at that moment a shot rang out.

The bullet caught blue tunic in the left eye and came out just above the left ear in a blossom of red speckled with white bone fragments and blobs of grey brain matter. Blue tunic spun around on his good leg before crashing to the ground, legs kicking.

The Comancheros stood frozen to the spot, just for an instant, no more than the blink of an eye. A second shot took another in the heart and threw him backwards to writhe in short-lived death throes on the ground. The rest ran for their mounts in panic. Another went down as a third bullet shattered his lower spine and blew a fist-sized exit hole in his stomach. The remaining three dived for the ground pulling rifles from their shoulders.

After the initial shock and surprise and as the others started running, Caleb launched himself forward to where blue tunic lay. He snatched up the rifle blue tunic had been using as a crutch. Adrenalin pumping, temporarily driving the pain from his aching limbs, Caleb came to his knees, firing at the three fleeing men, sending one to the ground, a bullet severing his spine.

The two remaining Comancheros turned and in a half-bent position began firing wildly at Caleb. Caleb dived sideways, rolled and came back on to his knees; his shots were not wild and a second man went down, writhing his death throes in the dust.

The last Comanchero threw his rifle aside and made one last effort to reach the now skittish horses. Before Caleb could fire the mysterious shootist sent the running man to the ground.

Caleb came to his feet and turned his gaze north, the direction in which his unknown saviour had fired and saved his life. He saw movement on the rimrock. A figure was standing and waving a rifle. Against the glare of the sky he could not make the figure out until a voice made thin by distance called, 'Caleb!'

Caleb's jaw dropped in surprise. It couldn't be.

'Caleb! It's me, Nathan!' the waving figure called.

Caleb stared in awe and wonder at the boy he had seen die. He hadn't the spit to shout back from his dry mouth, instead he waved to acknowledge he had heard Nathan's words and the figure on the rimrock vanished.

Caleb retrieved his rig from the dead blue tunic and he buckled it on. Then he scooped up the pistol the other had loaded, sliding it back into its holster before completing the reloading of the second pistol. He mentally gauged the distance from the rimrock to where he stood and shook his head in disbelief. Dammit, that boy was good!

While he waited for Nathan to join him, Caleb limped across to where a small stream appeared briefly beneath the northern escarpment just beyond where the collection of huts stood. He drank deeply from the stream and immersed his head to clear it before setting his mind to the next problem.

It took Nathan ten minutes to scramble down the cliff to reach Caleb. Caleb hugged the big youth, earning a grimace and yell from Nathan as the other squeezed his injured arm.

'Dammit, boy, how come you ain't dead? I saw you go over the edge mysel'.' And then, while Caleb cleaned up Nathan's wound and used his own bandanna to re-dress it, Nathan gave a run-down of events. Afterwards Caleb shook his head in wonder. 'If'n that don't beat all,' he breathed.

'Took me a time to find this place. Got mysel' lost a few times,' Nathan admitted ruefully. 'Folks were pulling out by the time I found my way here.'

'But find it you did, an' for that I'm

truly thankful. Them varmints were ready to do things that even I hadn't thought of.' Caleb gave a shudder.

'But the girls? What about the girls, sir,' Nathan asked anxiously.

'They were sold to a Colonel Salazar o' the Mexican army. Seems there's a fort a day's ride to the south. That's where they're being taken an' that's where we're heading now.'

'Take on the Mexican army?' Nathan howled in disbelief.

'I'd take on the whole o' Mexico if needs be,' Caleb replied darkly. 'Are you ready to ride? We need to head out now if'n we're to get there afore nightfall.'

'You look like you could do wi' some rest for a spell,' Nathan objected.

'I'll get all the rest I need when I'm dead. Before that, got me some girls that need a grandpa real bad. You game for taking on Salazar an' his men, boy?'

'I've come this far,' Nathan said stoutly.

'Can you ride bareback?' Caleb

inclined his head towards where the Comancheros' horses stood in a nervous group.

'That's how I learned to ride,' Nathan said.

'Take a look in the huts. See if'n there ain't something we can use for a trip in the desert. I'm gonna take a look at them dead fellas. Some extra fire-power might be useful. I'll meet you by the horses.' That said, Caleb limped away, wincing as he went.

'Found a canteen and filled it from the stream,' Nathan said as he joined Caleb ten minutes later, 'an' this.' He held out a bottle half-full of tequila. Caleb took it and studied it for a long moment.

'Nah!' he said tossing the bottle aside. 'In a way it was drink caused this whole damn mess. Made me leave my family, lost me my job. Wi' out it things might have turned out different.'

'You cain't blame yoursel', Caleb — ' Nathan began.

'Well I do,' Caleb snapped back.

'Now I intend to put things right. Found me a shotgun an' a pocketful o' twelve-guage. Here.' He tossed a shell-filled bandolier to Nathan. 'Shells for your rifle.' As Nathan slipped the bandolier over his neck and shoulder, Caleb continued, 'Sooner we get going, the sooner we'll be there an' the sooner we'll get them girls away. Find yoursel' a hat, them *hombres* won't be needing them agin, then pick a horse an' let's be on our way.'

'One o' their greasy hats?' Nathan said, aghast at the idea.

'Better than having the sun boil the brains in your skull,' Caleb cut back as he slung the shotgun by its crude, rawhide strap over his shoulder and swung himself astride a skittish pinto. 'Time's a-wasting, boy.'

★ ★ ★

The fort lay in the centre of a horseshoe-shaped range of low, scrub-covered sandy hills. Beyond the open end of the horseshoe a vast expanse of barren desert stretched to the southern horizon. Just now the sun was sinking rapidly in the west, bathing the area within the horseshoe in a Hadean glow and painting the white adobe walls of the fort red beneath a darkening blue sky.

The fort was a squat, ugly building of high, featureless walls, its only means of entry through a pair of thick wooden doors above which squatted a dome-topped lookout tower.

Caleb and Nathan were hunkered down behind a ridge of low sand dunes at the northern, closed end of the horseshoe. They had made good time, pushing their mounts hard, and Salazar and his men with the captive girls were barely thirty minutes ahead. From a distant hill they had seen them reach the fort. Now all they could do was keep out of sight until nightfall. From where they crouched they looked at the rear of the fort. Occasionally soldiers could be seen patrolling the ramparts.

'How we gonna get the girls away from there wi' out being seen?' Nathan asked worriedly. He turned his head to look at Caleb, who was now seated at the rear of the hollow, legs thrust out before him, fingers laced together across his stomach as though he hadn't a care in the world. Caleb gave a sniff.

'As I see it, in a situation like this, you gotta make the most of what you got.'

Nathan gave a snorting laugh. ''Pears to me that we ain't got anything.' He scowled at Caleb from beneath the brim of a battered black Stetson.

'Now that's where you're wrong, boy, an' it's what them damn Comancheros found out. Yessir!' Caleb nodded and Nathan looked puzzled.

'I ain't sure I'm with you, Caleb.'

'Surprise, boy, surprise,' Caleb explained. 'The last thing old Salazar is expecting is two dumb, dead gringos to be paying him a visit.'

'There were only six Comancheros,' Nathan pointed out.

'Six, sixty, six hundred, it don't make no difference,' Caleb said casually. 'Two men on their own can do more than two hundred.' He gave a nod.

'Reckon I'd feel a darn sight safer wi' two hundred men,' Nathan said with feeling.

Caleb gave a sigh. 'Let's say we had two hundred men. Ain't no way you can keep them hidden. You'd have to attack the fort, an' sitting up on those walls, them Mexicans would pick off every last man-jack, ain't no two ways 'bout it.' Caleb nodded at his own wisdom.

'I can see that,' Nathan was forced to agree.

'But you wouldn't see two men under cover of darkness sneaking into the fort until it was too late.'

'OK, we've snuck into the fort, what do we do now? Say hands up, you're under arrest?'

'Something like that,' Caleb agreed.

'Dammit, Caleb, you're fooling wi' me,' Nathan said angrily raising a

95

chuckle from the other.

'Just a tad, boy, just a tad, but just afore you go getting yoursel' all strung out, I'm willing to bet that somewhere in that fort is a magazine plumb full of explosives. They got kerosene lamps which means barrels o' oil. Mix the two together an'' — Caleb raised his hands and eyebrows — 'bang!'

Nathan stared at him with an almost glazed expression.

'Now I ain't saying it's gonna be easy,' Caleb continued. 'Lotta things could go wrong. Could be both o' us'll end up dead. Hell! There are so many things that could go wrong that it ain't worth spit worrying 'bout them, but remember: surprise, that's on our side. Anything else we take as it happens an' trust to luck we make the right decision at the time. Now, I'm jus' 'bout all talked out. Got any o' that jerky left?'

Night came quickly as they waited. The redness faded from the walls of the fort as purple shadows slid down the sides of the western hills and spread out across the sandy floor of the horseshoe basin, reaching out to meet the darkness that rushed in from the east.

Overhead the sky blackened and stars exploded into life casting a baleful, ghostly light over the fort, while from within the glow from many lamps cast a yellowish dome of light above the walls. A light breeze stirred the sand, blowing it through the scrub with a dry, hissing sound.

'Reckon it's time to go, boy. Are you ready?' Caleb said softly.

Nathan swallowed nervously, mouth suddenly dry.

''Bout as ready as I'll ever be,' he mumbled unhappily in reply.

In the darkness Caleb smiled. He put a hand on Nathan's shoulder.

'The girls are depending on us.'

6

The two made a crouching run to the rear wall of the fort. While Nathan flattened himself against it Caleb prepared the lasso that he had brought with him, looking up to locate his objective.

Circling the upper walls, a series of thick poles jutted a foot or so out. These formed part of the supports that held a wooden walkway three feet below the inner edge of the wall.

Caleb tossed the rope with practised ease. It snagged on one of the jutting supports and Caleb pulled to close the loop about the support. There seemed to be a lot of noise coming from the fort which was just as well, for Caleb's feet scraped against the wall, slipping a couple of times as he hauled himself up the twenty or so feet to the top and dropped on to the wooden walkway on the other side. Nathan quickly followed to join Caleb and together they crouched down, backs to the wall to stare down at the scene below.

'Goddamit!' Caleb breathed.

The compound within the fort was lit up by dozens of kerosene lamps. These were augmented by a series of burning braziers that threw flickering red shadows over the gathered throng and danced jerkily around the walls. The braziers surrounded a central platform upon which three Indians were spread-eagled upright to a stout, wooden frame. Their arms were above their heads, bound to the crosspiece above their heads by their wrists; their legs were spread, with ankles tied to iron spikes driven into the platform base so that each man formed an X shape.

The two outer figures were drenched in blood, the flesh of their naked torsos flayed off by a whip. Their heads lolled forward on to their mutilated chests and by the way they hung Caleb could see that they were dead.

The central figure was still alive, a magnificent specimen of a man wearing only a loincloth. His chest, arms and legs were deeply muscled, but even his muscles could not break the bonds that held him. All he could do was glare with proud defiance at his tormentors as he waited for the same ending that had taken his two companions.

Nathan stared with wide, horrified eyes at the scene before him. It reminded him of the visions of hell conjured up by the Reverend Blake in his Sunday sermons, and he shuddered.

Soldiers and civilians rubbed shoulders, drink bringing them together as equals. They talked, joked, laughed and got even drunker. The smell of food cooking was heavy on the air. Everyone seemed to be having a good time.

A second, smaller platform containing a padded chair that had probably graced a hotel at some time, stood a few yards from the central platform. The chair was unoccupied but Caleb surmised it was for Salazar.

'What's going on, Caleb?' Nathan whispered.

'Some sort o' fiesta. Guess them poor souls are the entertainment.' Caleb's face was grim. 'Reckon Salazar could teach them Comancheros a thing or two 'bout torture an' death.' As he finished speaking he changed position until he was belly down on the walkway, his head jutting over the inner edge to get a better view.

Below them, flush to the wall, ran a series of buildings, most likely the officers' quarters. Against the eastern side wall was another long building: the soldiers' bunkhouse. Against the western wall the buildings were fewer and huddled in one corner. Next to them lay a long corral where horses milled about restlessly and next to that an open-fronted stable block. But it was a building standing on its own beyond the stables that caught Caleb's eye: a squat, windowless building. A smile touched Caleb's lips before he continued his visual search of the fort's

101

interior. The southern wall contained the huge double gates with the lookout tower above it. The lookout was missing, as were the guards who had patrolled the walls earlier; probably down in the compound getting liquored up.

To finish his visual inspection he noted that stout wooden poles supported the encircling walkway every twenty or so feet, like the cloisters of a church.

Caleb had not expected the crowd that milled about below. Must have been a hundred or more, three-quarters of them soldiers. The civilians were probably the cooks and cleaners and general servants attached to the fort. Caleb resumed his position in the deeper shadows at the wall edge of the walkway.

'Sure is a lotta folks 'bout,' Nathan observed nervously.

'Mebbe that's in our favour. Less likely to be seen, an' the way them boys are drinking, they ain't likely to see anything. Reckon I've got the magazine spotted. That building on its own at the far end just past the stable. No windows, standing on its own. Gotta be it.' He nodded. It was the building that had made him smile earlier.

'How 'bout where the girls are being kept?'

'This end o' the corral, I reckon, under the walkway. Need to get a proper look. Follow me an' keep low.'

The two made their way to where a set of wooden steps led down to the ground, giving access to the walkway that they were now on and the one around the perimeter of the west wall.

Crouched near to the top of the steps, Caleb whispered, 'I can just make out the top of a metal gate that I figure is the fort prison.'

'What do we do?'

A tight smile played over Caleb's features.

'What this little party needs is a few fireworks to liven it up. I'm going for the magazine. You stay here, belly to the floor. If'n anything goes wrong I might be in need of you an' your rifle. Now, when all hell breaks loose, get yoursel' down to the prison an' get the girls out. You'll probably have to shoot the lock out. Don' worry 'bout me, I'll find you an' then we'll get the hell outta here. You reckon you can do that?'

Nathan nodded. 'I won't let you down, Caleb.'

'I know you won't, boy. I'm depending on you an' so are the girls.' Caleb cast Nathan an encouraging smile, then rose up and moved quickly down the wooden steps. To Nathan's ears the sound of Caleb's boots was like a rapid and loud drum roll.

At the other three corners of the fort, wide wooden steps gave access to the walkways. These were supplemented by five more sets, three midway along the walls with another two either side of the entrance gates. Caleb reached the bottom of the steps and vanished down them into the shadows below leaving Nathan feeling very alone and vulnerable.

A sudden cheer went up from the drunken throats below, making Nathan start. For an instant he thought that Caleb had been discovered, but it was only the appearance of Salazar. Flanked by two of his lieutenants he made his way to the raised chair and settled himself in it like a king on a throne. The one-eyed man, his back to the prone Nathan, eyed the Indian with his one bright eye and a hush settled over the gathered people. The sudden silence made Nathan hold his breath. His rapidly beating heart, pressed to the boards of the walkway, filled his ears with its drumming. It seemed so loud that he expected eyes to be turned in his direction.

Salazar rubbed the scarred flesh over his blind eye.

'The last time we met, Red Shirt of the Comanches, you took my eye. For that . . . I will take your life as I have taken the lives of your brothers. But before that you will watch as my men take your squaw wife.'

At that a second cheer went up from the crowd, this time more prolonged and accompanied by many of the men pulling guns and firing them into the air.

Caleb, who had pressed himself into the shadows between the stable block and the building he took to be the magazine, moved as the cheer went up. In the frenzy of the shouting and gunfire, his own shot that blew out the lock of building door, went unnoticed. He darted in and closed the door, sniffing the air. In the darkness a smile spread across his face, for the air was thick with the pungent smell of kerosene and he knew his guess about the building had been right. He fished a lucifer from his pocket and thumbed it into sputtering life, raising it above his head.

Beside half a dozen barrels of oil there were kegs of gunpowder, boxes full of ammunition, crates of dynamite and coils of fuse wire. He found a lamp and after standing it on a barrel of oil, lit it, probably not the cleverest thing to do in such an explosive atmosphere, but he needed to see what he was doing. He turned the wick down to its lowest level and set to work.

In his chair, Salazar eyed the impassive face of Red Shirt, seeing the hate burning deep within the Indian's eyes.

'Bring out the squaw,' Salazar called out loudly and a third cheer, louder and longer than the first two, filled the air and pistols were emptied at the sky in anticipation of what was to come.

Caleb placed the lamp on the floor and took the opportunity to knock in the lids of the barrels. He was almost ready to leave. His pockets were stuffed with sticks of dynamite bound together with twine in bundles of five, the centre stick of each primed with a short length of fuse. All that was left to do was to attach a longer length of fuse leading to the crates of dynamite. This he did. He had no way of knowing how fast the fuse would burn. He just hoped it would give him enough time to get clear. He was about to light the fuse when the door crashed open.

Emilio Lopez had not meant to enter the magazine store. Until the first cheer went up announcing Salazar's appearance he had been sleeping off the effects of too much drink in the darkness next to the far end of the store. By the time the third cheer erupted with the accompaniment of gunfire, Emilio had staggered as far as the magazine store door. He paused in the doorway, back to the door, to take another pull at his bottle but, in tipping his head back to pour the fiery liquid down his throat, he overbalanced and fell against the door.

With the lock shot away the door opened easily and Emilio went sprawling on to his back on the floor of the magazine. The fall blew the breath from his body and the back of his head smacked the floor painfully hard.

Stars danced before his eyes against a yellow background, then the face of a gringo floated before his dazed eyes.

'Real neighbourly o' you to drop in, *amigo*,' the face said and that was the last he remembered as Caleb slammed the barrel of a Colt against Emilio's temple. The stars went out and the yellow glow turned black.

Caleb extinguished the lamp and risked a quick look outside to see if anyone had seen the glow of the lamp from outside, but everyone's attention was centred on the middle of the compound.

With just the light from outside to work by, Caleb lit the fuse and blew the lucifer out. Never one to miss an opportunity and take advantage of the unexpected, Caleb hoisted Emilio up and with Emilio's left arm pulled across his shoulder and his right arm around Emilio's waist he went out of the magazine store, leaving behind a spluttering, hissing flame of the burning fuse. Taking just a few seconds to pull the door to, Caleb moved as quickly as he could away from the magazine store. The direction Caleb was taking put

Emilio on the side closest to the crowd, thereby shielding himself.

The noise from the crowd grew louder as a striking-looking Indian woman was dragged unceremoniously before Salazar. Her hands were bound behind her back as she was forced to her knees before Salazar. Salazar rose to his feet, raised his arms for silence and the crowd grew quiet.

Salazar dropped back into the chair, his single eye fixed on Red Shirt.

'You can save your woman from much pain. All you have to do is tell me where your tribe is hiding.'

The woman raised her head, looked over her shoulder at Red Shirt and snapped out words in her own language. Salazar did not know what was said, but he could hazard a guess that she was telling her man not to say anything.

'I will find them some day,' Salazar pointed out.

'But not from my lips,' Red Shirt said. 'What are the lives of two for a hundred?' There was almost a sneer in his voice.

Salazar leaned forward, a vicious look on his face.

'Then before you die, Indian, listen to the screams of your woman. Hear her beg. That will be the sound you take to your grave.' He raised his voice. 'Soldiers of Salazar, the woman is yours!'

A roar of approval went up from the waiting men and at the same time the magazine store exploded.

In a massive, thunderous explosion the magazine store ceased to exist, as did a section of the fort wall behind it.

Caleb threw himself flat as pieces of the adobe walls flew out across the compound from within a dense cloud of rising, spreading, black smoke, followed by barrels of oil that cartwheeled against the night sky. They threw out streamers of blazing liquid that fell as burning rain on the people below.

Panic swept through the crowd, turning their cheers to screams of terror. They scattered, blundering into each other and stamping on those who had fallen, hit by the flying debris from the exploding store. To add confusion to the nightmare the terrified horses broke through the corral fence and stampeded into the scattering crowd.

The explosion galvanized Nathan into action. He clattered down the wooden steps two at a time. A stunned soldier appeared at the bottom of the steps, looking up at the approaching figure. He just had time to register surprise a second time in a few, short seconds before the butt of Nathan's rifle pole-axed him to the ground. A few quick steps later Nathan was at the barred gate of the prison block.

'Ellie, Katie,' he called anxiously into the darkness within. A pale face, ringed with matted golden hair appeared on the other side of the gate and fingers gripped the bars.

'Nathan, Nathan is that you?' There was disbelief in the girl's voice and eyes.

'It's me all right,' he assured her.

'What's happening?' she asked, as smaller explosions from sticks of dynamite ignited by the initial blast were blown across the compound and rocked the fort.

A grim smile tweaked Nathan's lips. 'Your grandpa's happening. Now, get everyone back agin the side wall, I'm gonna shoot out the lock.'

Caleb came to his feet as the oil barrels fell to earth, splitting apart on impact and sending rivers of fire across the compound, turning running figures into human torches. One barrel reached the far wall, breaking apart as it hit the wooden walkway and forming a blazing waterfall that cascaded on to the roof of the barracks block below.

Caleb jumped up on to the platform and moved swiftly towards Red Shirt, pulling a knife as he went. The Indian struggled against his bonds, trying to look over his shoulder as he heard Caleb.

'Take it easy, boy. I ain't here to kill you. Name's Caleb Jones.' As he spoke Caleb moved in front of Red Shirt and slashed the wrist bonds, then the ankle bonds. A scream made Caleb turn. A fat Mexican soldier stood behind the Indian woman, who was still on her knees. He was pulling her head back by the hair with one hand and wielding a knife in the other. Caleb drew, left-handed, and fired.

'That ain't no way to treat a lady,' he roared as the bullet made a tiny hole in the man's forehead, but blew the back of his head out as it exited in a blossom of blood, bone and brain.

Red Shirt had fallen to his knees, his ankles temporarily refusing to take his weight. Caleb leapt down from the platform, hauled the woman to her feet and sliced through the hopes that bound her wrists.

'Help your man,' he said as a bullet hummed like an angry hornet past his left ear. He spun, dropping the knife and going for both pistols as three Mexican soldiers rushed towards him, pistols drawn, firing wildly. Caleb's aim was not wild and the three soldiers dropped.

Red Shirt, the feeling back in wrists and ankles, had dropped down from the platform. Caleb holstered one pistol and pulled another from the holster of the man who had tried to kill the woman. He tossed it to Red Shirt.

'Get your woman away from here. Got me some females o' my own to rescue. Good luck. I hope you make it.' With that Caleb turned and ran towards the prison block. He paused once at a glowing brazier, lighting the fuses of two dynamite bundles. He tossed one towards the barracks block, the other at the officers' quarters before completing his run to the prison block. There he found Nathan standing protectively with five girls in tow.

Relief was evident on the young man's face at the sight of Caleb charging through the swirling eddies of smoke and dust. As Caleb reached Nathan the two charges he had thrown exploded noisily one after the other. One blew in the walls of the barracks block, the other destroyed the entrance to the officers' quarters.

'I'm mighty pleased to see you, sir,' Nathan greeted.

'Feeling's mutual, boy. You done a good job.'

'Grandpa!' Ellie, with Katie in tow, ran forward and hugged the old man. Caleb, after a couple of seconds, disengaged himself from their grip.

'Didn't think I'd leave you here, did you?' Caleb raised eyebrows in mock surprise.

'I knew you'd come for us, Grandpa,' Katie said solemnly.

'Girl should allus believe in her grandpa,' Caleb said. 'But right now we need to get outta here an' get you safe.'

'Can Rachel, Molly an' Sally come with us, Grandpa?' Katie asked, looking towards the three newcomers.

'Are you the Baker girls?' Caleb asked remembering hearing about a wagon being attacked just before Ellie and Katie were taken.

The tallest of the girls nodded. 'Yes, sir.'

'You're more than welcome to come along. Like I said, we need to move now, afore what passes for soldiers in these parts get the notion to regroup. Figure Salazar is still alive.' He eyed Nathan. 'He was gone by the time I cut that Indian loose; gone to ground I reckon, but he'll be back. Nathan, you follow on behind an' I'll lead. Keep your eyes open for any soldier boys who may be feeling brave enough to be soldiers agin. Let's go!' With that he led them across the now deserted compound to the gates of the fort, which were wide open as the people within sought to escape the burning hell that had suddenly engulfed them, and led them out into the night.

7

Salazar emerged from the wrecked officers' quarters, where he had fled to escape the rain of fire. His clothes were blackened and torn, blood oozed from a cut on his right cheekbone, but he paid it little heed as he stared around at the death and destruction that confronted him.

The walkways around the walls were ablaze. Flames leapt from the stable block and the barracks block. The compound was littered with bodies. Those who still stood drifted as aimlessly as the acrid smoke that swirled around them. There was a splintering crash off to one side. He turned his head in time to see the walkway above the barracks block sag and then fall, crashing on to the roof below in a shower of sparks.

A soldier, hatless and bloodied,

staggered coughing from the flame-stained smoke. He stopped before Salazar and snapped a salute.

'The prisoners are gone, Colonel,' he said voice harsh from inhaled smoke, eyes red and watering.

'Thomas said it was a young gringo who led them away. A second gringo, older, was seen cutting the Indian free. I do not know, I did not see,' he added hastily.

Salazar stared at the man with his single eye. But Salazar had seen. He had seen a 'dead' man cut Red Shirt free before the swirling smoke had obscured his vision. Aguilar's prisoner in the cage. A man called Caleb Jones! That one gringo — no, two gringos, if the soldier's report was to be believed, should be responsible for this carnage and destruction seemed inconceivable, but that was how it appeared.

Caleb Jones! His hands balled and flexed at his sides in suppressed anger. Aguilar would pay dearly for allowing the man to live!

'What are your orders, Colonel,' the soldier asked nervously and Salazar turned a cold eye coloured red by the flames glowing on the man.

'Gather what men are still standing and find the horses,' he snapped harshly.

Caleb met with no opposition as he led his small party away from the fort, heading back to the low, sandy hills where they had left their horses. He was worried that the horses might have bolted during the explosions, but they were still in the hollow where they had been left and, to his surprise, had been joined by a third horse. Probably one that had stampeded from the fort.

Having the extra horse made all the difference. Ellie could travel with Nathan, Katie with him and the three Baker girls on the extra mount. Caleb and Nathan gathered their few belongings, which they had hidden in the scrub: the canteen of water, Nathan's shoulder-bag with its meagre rations of jerky, the bandolier and Caleb's shotgun. Then, by the light of a thin crescent moon which had now risen, Caleb led the group north. He was in no doubt that Salazar, once he could muster his men and round up the horses, would be on their trail, so he needed to put as much distance as possible between themselves and the fort.

Their passage through the horseshoe hills was quick to begin with, Caleb pushing the pace, but once they reached the cliffs and began to climb the steep trail the pace slowed.

The trail was narrow and in places dropped away sheer on one side into invisible ravines, their depths hidden by the darkness.

It was madness to continue riding through the intense shadows with the high cliffs preventing the moonlight from reaching the trail. In the end it was a combination of the cold and dark that forced Caleb to call a halt and make camp. The girls in their thin dresses, with no outer garments to protect them from the cold, were shivering. In a small hollow off the trail,

Caleb gathered dry brush and made a small fire which the girls gathered around as close as they dared, pushing hands towards the crackling flames.

Nathan gave his jacket to the Baker girls to huddle under as best they could, while Ellie snuggled up to him. Katie sat with Caleb wrapped in Caleb's coat. The firelight danced over their faces as they chewed the last of the jerky.

'Won't they see the fire, Grandpa?' Ellie asked.

'They won't come looking for us till dawn,' Caleb said.

'Can you be sure o' that, sir?' Nathan asked.

'Pretty much. It'll take Salazar time to round up his men an' horses, probably the best part o' the night. He knows we can't travel fast so he'll wait until first light an' then come fast. He won't risk riding that trail in the dark. Say, how you girls doing? Getting warm?'

'Yes, sir,' three voices came in unison.

They lapsed into silence. Katie looked up into Caleb's face.

'Has Mama gone to see Jesus, Grandpa?' she asked in a small, quivering voice.

A lump rose in Caleb's throat.

'Yes, button. She's wi' Jesus now, looking down on us an' keeping us safe,' he murmured, hugging her close.

'How will she keep us safe, Grandpa?'

'Hush, Katie,' Ellie called across, a catch in her voice.

'Who will look after us, Grandpa?'

'Why, I will, darling, that's what grandpas are for.'

'What about Rachel, Molly an' Sally?' Katie wanted to know. 'Will you be their grandpa?'

'That's enough, Katie,' Ellie said sharply.

'Reckon they may well have a grandpa o' their own. Till then I'll be looking after you all. Now you go an' sit wi' your sister, I need to speak to Nathan.'

'Nathan an' Ellie are sparking, Grandpa,' Katie said in a loud whisper.

'Katie! For goodness sake,' Ellie said angrily.

'That's why I need to speak to

Nathan afore the pair o' them catch on fire. Now off you go an' share that coat wi' Ellie.' Caleb rose stiffly to his feet. 'You girls try an' get some sleep, now.'

'My tummy's rumbling,' Katie called out.

'An' there's me thinking it was thunder,' Caleb returned and earned himself a giggle from Katie as Nathan joined him. The two walked to the edge of the camp before Caleb spoke again.

'Ain't gonna be much rest for we 'uns, boy. Need to take turns keeping a watch during the night.'

'I thought you said Salazar wouldn't come at night,' Nathan challenged.

'It ain't Salazar I'm concerned with. I don' reckon them Comancheros we met t'other day were on their own. Could be there's more out there looking for revenge.'

Nathan nodded. 'I'd clean forgotten 'bout them fellas,' he admitted. 'So what do we do, Caleb?'

'Two-hour watches through the night. I'll take the first watch an' I'll come an' get you when it's your turn, then it's back to me. We do that till first light. OK?'

'OK, Caleb,' Nathan agreed.

Despite his worries the night passed without disturbances. As first light filtered to them from the east Caleb was leading the tired, hungry party out.

★ ★ ★

At the same time as Caleb broke camp Salazar was heading a column of twenty of his toughest men away from the gutted fort, leaving the remainder, with a contingent of civilians, to guard and clear up the fort, bury the dead and look after the injured. Just now his thoughts were with the man called Caleb Jones and his companion, the ones responsible for the death and destruction at the fort, and vengeance burned in his heart. They would not escape the wrath of Salazar.

★ ★ ★

It was close to noon when a bullet took down the horse the Baker girls were riding, sending the three shrieking and sprawling to the ground. It had been a frustratingly slow ride for Caleb, with the horses bearing extra weight. They were passing through an open canyon, wide at the top and narrow at the bottom with high, steeply sloping walls on either side, when they came upon the mine.

They had reached an area where the canyon bottom widened, the western slope receding back to form an open semicircle a hundred yards wide and as much deep, partly choked with scrub. The entrance to the mine lay at the back of the depression, a dark, timber-framed rectangle that led back into the cliff face.

'Looks deserted,' Nathan opined to Caleb.

'Sure don' look as though it'd been worked in a coon's age,' Caleb agreed. Scrub grew in the mine entrance. 'Reckon it's an old, played-out silver mine,' he mused. That was when the shot rang out.

Caleb wheeled his horse, drawing a pistol. The shot had come from the eastern slope. His eyes raked the scrub oak dotted slope, its top marked with weathered, broken rocks like rotten teeth. He caught sight of a crouching, uniformed soldier, a rifle to his shoulder. Hampered as he was, holding on to Katie, he thumbed off two quick shots. The rifleman gave a cry and toppled forward, sliding down the slope which was covered with a layer of gravel-like scree weathered from the rocks above, until he caught in a patch of tenaciously clinging scrub and hung there lifelessly beneath a swirl of slowly settling brown dust.

The Baker girls were coming to their feet, panic, fear and confusion filling their terrified faces.

'Get to the mine!' Caleb roared at them as he slid from his mount clutching Katie under one arm. In the meantime Nathan had dropped down from his horse and with Ellie in tow made a crouching run to where the Baker girls were standing in confusion. He herded them towards the mine entrance, leaving it up to Ellie to take them there while he remained behind to help Caleb.

A second shot came from above. Nathan's horse gave a harsh whinny and reared up, pawing the air before crashing to the ground.

Caleb ran with Katie to where Nathan crouched rifle in hand scanning the canyon rim for signs of movement. He pushed Katie down behind a scrub thicket before dropping to one knee and scanning the eastern rim with Nathan.

'See anything?' Caleb asked.

'Nothin' to get a bead on,' Nathan replied.

There was movement up there, but this time the attackers were keeping low, giving him nothing to shoot at.

A third shot from the rim sent Caleb's mount to the ground where it lay thrashing its legs, bloody foam erupting from its nostrils, as the life drained from it.

'It is a long ride to Border Town, Señor Jones, but it is an even longer walk.' Salazar's voice, tinged with amusement, floated down to them.

'Show yoursel', Salazar, or are you too lily-livered to face an old man, a boy an' a bunch o' unarmed girls?' Caleb goaded. 'Is that how Mexican soldiers fight?' The goad became a jeer as he tried to draw them out into showing themselves.

'You have no food or water, Señor Jones and now no horses. Not a good situation to be in. Don't you agree, gringo?'

'He's right, Caleb,' Nathan said softly, casting Caleb a worried glance.

'As my ol' pa said, 'It ain't no use worrying 'til it happens.' '

Nathan's eyebrows arched. 'Looks to me like it has happened,' he pointed out.

Caleb gave a bleak smile. 'Not yet. We're still alive, ain't we?'

'You could, of course, throw down your weapons and give yourselves up,' Salazar's voice broke over them again, 'but in view of your recent actions — the killing of Mexican soldiers, destruction of property belonging to the government of Mexico — both actions carrying the death penalty, you do not, as you Americanos say, have a leg to stand on.'

Caleb frowned. 'You are trying to jaw us to death, Salazar?'

'Just pointing out the futility of your situation, Señor Jones. There is no escape for you.' From the sound of his voice, Salazar was enjoying himself.

'Go to hell, Salazar!' Caleb roared back.

'I think you will get there before me, Señor Jones.'

''Member another gent being o' the same opinion. He was wrong,' Caleb returned.

'Caleb, they're coming!' Nathan called out urgently as a distant drumming of galloping hoofs sounded in the canyon from the direction they themselves had come.

'Get Katie to the mine,' Caleb snapped out, digging into the pockets of his coat.

'But — ' Nathan began.

'Now ain't the time to argue, boy. Do it!' Caleb shouted as a a wave of riders appeared around a bend. They were riding fast and bent forward low in the saddle. Nathan bit back the words of protest that were forming on his lips. Rifle in hand, he darted to where Katie was crouched, picked her up under one arm and raced for the mine entrance.

There was movement up on the eastern ridge, suggesting to Caleb that once the riders were in a position to start shooting their comrades on the ridge would join in. Extracting a last fused bundle of dynamite sticks which he had not used at the fort, he found a lucifer, thumbed it into life and applied it to the fuse. The fuse spluttered into hissing life. The riders were near now. He tossed the bundle into their path and threw himself flat.

The resultant explosion drowned out the crackle of rifle fire from the ridge. A fountain of sand and smoke erupted high into the air. The approaching riders were far enough away not to be caught in the blast but near enough for the animals they rode to be spooked by the thunderous explosion, which had been Caleb's intention, sending the animals veering and bucking, crashing into each other and throwing the riders from their saddles.

Caleb was up and running as a wave of dust, radiating out at ground level, propelled by the force of the blast, engulfed him. It almost took his legs out from under him but he managed to stay upright, clutching his hat to his head, and kept on running. He heard the sound of rifles, but the shooters on the ridge were firing blind into a pall of thick, brown dust that hid the running figure.

At Nathan's side, in the entrance to the mine, Ellie clapped a hand to her mouth in horror. The ground shook beneath their feet. Stone fragments fell from above, dislodged by the vibration of the blast.

'Grandpa!' she mouthed through her fingers.

Nathan, a sick feeling in his stomach at the thought that Caleb might have blown himself up, felt a wave of elation sweep over him as a figure staggered from the dust cloud.

'He's OK,' he yelled as Caleb lunged for the mine entrance spitting grit, his eyes stinging and watering from the scouring effect of the dust.

'Thought you'd killed yoursel',' Nathan gasped as Caleb staggered in and went to his knees, hands on his thighs, arms stiff, supporting his upper body from toppling forward sucking air into his labouring lungs as everyone crowded around, happy to see him.

'Was wondering mesel',' Caleb gasped hoarsely, coughing. 'Dammit! I'm too old for this.' He twisted himself into a sitting position back against the wall, rubbing the tears from his eyes.

'Here, Grandpa.' Ellie thrust a canteen into Caleb's hands. Caleb took a mouthful and then handed it back. It was warm and brackish, but it seemed to him to be the finest water he had ever tasted.

Katie flung herself on to Caleb's lap and hugged him before casting a proud look at the Baker girls.

'Didn't I say he was the best grandpa in the world?'

The brief respite of the reunion was short-lived. There was the crunch of boots on loose scree outside. Nathan whirled around at a half-crouch, rifle at waist level, ready to use.

Something flew into the mine at an angle. It hit the wall and fell to the ground. A single primed stick of dynamite with less than an inch of spluttering fuse to go.

'Nathan, *noooo!*' Ellie gave a shrill, agonized cry as the young man darted forward. There was no time to pick up the dynamite and throw it out for already the burning fuse had reached the end of the stick. Instead he kicked it, then turned and threw himself flat, hands to his ears.

The dynamite stick was passing out through the entrance when it exploded sending shock waves racing into the mine, making the walls tremble and showering dust down on to the cowering group from cracks in the ceiling.

Dust surged and billowed over him, then, as the last echoes of the explosion faded away in the dark depths of the mine an ominous creaking and groaning filled the air. A loud, splintering cracking sound came from the entrance of the mine. Nathan rolled over and peered back through the thinning dust in time to see the heavy, wooden lintel of the door frame sag. It was accompanied by harsh grating sound.

'Run, boy! The mine's collapsing,' Caleb yelled.

Nathan was up and running deeper into the mine towards the others when, with a rumble like thunder, the roof around the entrance caved in and the small amount of light filtering through the entrance vanished to be replaced by an inky, choking blackness pierced by the terrified screaming of the girls.

They were trapped!

8

A feeling of panic washed over Nathan, drying his mouth and setting his heart racing. The thought of being trapped in the awful darkness terrified him. Then to his relief a lucifer flared in the darkness and pale, frightened faces sprang into being.

'Dammit, boy, that was a fool thing to do,' Caleb snapped out. 'Coulda got yoursel' blowed up.' Caleb's face looked ferocious in the flickering, yellow light, then suddenly a smile stretched his lips. 'But I figure if'n you hadn't then a lot more o' this mine woulda come down.'

'Nathan.' Ellie rushed across and hugged Nathan. 'You scared me so,' she said, burying her face in his chest, much to his embarrassment at such an open show of affection. He stood there, arms partly raised, unable to decide whether it was proper to return the hug. Luckily Caleb saved the situation.

'For goodness' sake, hold your intended, boy,' he thundered, amused by the other's show of propriety after all they'd been through.

As Nathan's arms went around Ellie's trembling body, Caleb gave a muted curse as the lucifer flame reached his fingers. He dropped it and the darkness flooded back, thicker and heavier than before.

The cloying darkness was not silent. Stone fragments clattered down the walls, making a hollow, clicking sound that mingled with the stealthy, furtive, grating rasp of stone against stone overlaid with tiny, explosive cracks of stressed rock.

To Caleb's mind they were not good sounds, but something had caught his eye just prior to the lucifer going out. Now he thumbed another into life. He always carried a supply of lucifers, but his stock was dwindling fast. As the lucifer flared into life Caleb's eyes settled on a niche set in the left-hand wall. Some five feet wide and reaching from floor to roof with a depth of about three feet, the shallow recess was stacked with wooden crates and barrels and tools: a couple of pickaxes and spades, along with some wooden buckets. Before the light went out he caught a glimpse of a crude shelf, the width of the recess. On it were two battered and dusty kerosene lamps. Caleb hurriedly lit another lucifer and three strides took him to the recess. Nathan moved to Caleb's side while Ellie organized the girls.

'Well, what have we here?' Caleb breathed. One of the wooden crates had been broken into pieces. Caleb bent and retrieved a foot-long fragment, two inches wide, which narrowed to a point. Holding the fragment by the narrow end he applied the almost spent flame to the other end.

The wood was tinder-dry and had probably lain there for years. It caught easily before he was forced to drop the lucifer.

As the fire took a hold and the light it threw off grew, Nathan eyed the clutter within the shallow recess before throwing Caleb a glance.

'What is this place?'

'Stash o' supplies for the mine. Check the lamps for oil.'

'Empty,' Nathan said after shaking the lamps.

'How 'bout the barrels?'

'Nothing,' Nathan replied disgustedly after a few minutes. 'Dry as a bone.' He knocked against a trio of stacked wooden crates and they toppled over with a crash. One contained half a dozen thick wooden sticks, tree-branches about eighteen inches long. Caleb stared down at them and a smile crossed his face.

'We may beat Salazar yet,' he murmured, retrieving one of the sticks. One end was thickly padded with a piece of rotting cloth wrapped around a bundle of leaves and small twigs tightly bound in position by thin strands of wire. 'Yes indeed,' Caleb breathed. He touched the flame from his piece of wooden crate to the padded end of the stick. It caught immediately and a bright, dancing flame pushed the darkness around them back.

'Torches to work by when they ran outta oil. Get 'em, Nathan, an' let's move on afore any more o' this tunnel comes down.'

With Caleb leading, Nathan brought up the rear while Ellie and Rachel, the eldest of the Baker girls, organized the three younger girls, Katie, Molly and Sally. Rachel, the same age as Ellie, dark-haired and pretty beneath the grime and dirt that coated them all, seemed used to taking care of her younger sisters. Caleb had divided the torches between himself and Nathan. Both carried a lighted one so the group were bathed in a coccoon of flickering light.

They had progressed a hundred or so yards down the mine tunnel when from behind came a low, drawn-out rumble that made the ground beneath their feet tremble. Caleb came to a halt, looking

141

back into the darkness beyond Nathan.

'Reckon that's more o' the tunnel collapsed,' he opined grimly. His words brought a whimper of fear from the younger girls.

'Hush, Molly, Sally,' Rachel jumped in quickly. 'We'll find another way out. Isn't that so, Mr Jones?' There was fear in the older girl's eyes, but she kept it from her voice.

Caleb sniffed. 'Seems to me that I've spent a whole lifetime getting outta situations that seemed plumb impossible at the time. This is just another one. I never gave up on them an' I sure ain't giving up on this one. When it's time for me to go, I aim to be sitting in a rocker looking at the setting sun. Down here there ain't no rocker an' no setting sun, so I suggest we go an' find 'em. You buttons don' be scared none. Do as your sister an' Ellie say an' we'll be fine.' He looked at Nathan and Nathan nodded. 'Let's move on then. Jus' you young'uns pretend it's night an' we'll go an' find the dawn.'

Caleb's words had a settling effect on the younger girls and as they progressed down the tunnel he could hear them chattering amongst themselves.

The tunnel proved to be about half a mile long. It ended abruptly in a chamber some ten foot wide and twice as deep. Gouges in the walls on either side showed evidence of pick marks. A pick and shovel rested against one wall, along with some more made-up torches. A spent torch had been wedged into a crack in the end wall where the mine tunnel merged with the chamber. Caleb pulled it out and jammed another in its place, lighting it from his own.

'We'll rest a spell here,' he announced, at the same time praying that the 'rest' would not be a permanent one. He moved deeper into the chamber holding the torch aloft. The roof of the chamber was much higher than the mine tunnel and, as more areas of the chamber came into view, he realized that the chamber was a natural cave.

As he moved deeper the flickering

light of the torch chased shadows before it and across the ceiling, which was gradually angling down to meet the floor at the rear of the chamber.

At one time water must have seeped into the chamber, for at the narrowed rear of the chamber, appearing ghostly in the light of the torch, a series of white, thin-waisted columns rose from mounds of smooth, rippled stone that reminded Caleb of candlewax that had melted and then hardened. He was looking at the awesome and beautiful sight of thousands of years of rock formation; the columns were the result of stalactite and stalagmite merging together running two, sometimes three rows deep from one side of the chamber to the other.

Stalactites of varying length hung like pointed spearheads between the columns, reaching down in vain for rising stalagmites in a union of stone that would never happen. For wherever the source of the water that had created these wonders had come from, it had long since dried up.

By now the others had joined Caleb and were staring, open-mouthed at the sight. Nathan passed his torch across to Ellie so the girls could have their own source of light, then he moved to Caleb's side, who had drifted to the right.

'Ain't looking too good is it, Caleb?' Nathan kept his voice low so the girls would not hear.

'Looks ain't everything, boy, but she sure smells real fine,' Caleb responded enigmatically, earning a puzzled scowl from the other. 'Yessir! Real fine,' Caleb ended in a murmur as he moved further from the now chattering girls, whose words were punctuated by giggles, their minds temporarily taken off the dire situation they were in.

'I ain't sure I'm following you, Caleb.'

'Use your nose, boy. The air smells a lot sweeter in here than it has a right to, an' a mite cooler too. Now what does that say to you?'

'That fresh air is getting in,' Nathan replied hopefully.

'An' if'n fresh air can get in, mebbe we can get out,' Caleb concluded. 'It's just a case o' finding out where.' Ten minutes later they found the opening, a dark, uninviting hole hidden behind the rippled mounds and columns, which appeared to drop straight down. Even more intriguing were the metal hooks driven into the rock on the edge of the hole, attached to which was a rope ladder.

'Why would someone put a rope ladder here?' Nathan turned his gaze on Caleb.

Caleb shrugged. 'Why indeed? Mebbe it leads to another silver lode?' he surmised. 'Mebbe just another way to get into the mine from a different direction? Or could be the mine workers were sending half the ore out one way an' the other half this way.'

Nathan peered down into the depths then gave a cry of surprise.

'Caleb, move the torch. I think I can

see light down there,' he said excitedly.

'The devil you say!' Moving the torch that he had been holding over the hole to one side Caleb peered down. The flickering light of the torch had prevented him from seeing the pale, diffused glow some thirty feet below him and as his eyes adjusted he could just make out the bottom few rungs of the rope ladder. 'This could be our way outta here.'

'I think I can hear something.' Nathan cocked his head to one side. Caleb did likewise. It was a low, continual hissing sound.

'That's water on the move,' Caleb declared, nodding his head and looking at Nathan. ''Member that river at the bottom o' the canyon?'

'Ain't likely to forget it,' Nathan replied with a shudder.

'The water down there could well be that same river. I reckon we've found our way out, boy. Hey, girls! Get over here.'

'How do we know the rope ladder is

safe, Grandpa?' It was Ellie who asked the question after the initial excitement of the possible way out abated.

'Reckon there's only one way,' Caleb drawled casually.

'That's right, an' I'd be obliged if'n you'd let me do the finding out,' Nathan spoke up.

Caleb nodded at the determined look on Nathan's face and pulled the lasso that was coiled about his upper body over his head. 'Get your arms through the loop so that if anything does happen we'll be able to haul you back.'

Nathan did as he was bid before seating himself on the edge of the hole, his legs dangling down.

'Be careful, Nathan,' Ellie implored.

'That I aim to be,' Nathan replied. Then, with thumping heart, he twisted around, got his feet on a rung of the rope ladder and started the descent, Caleb feeding out the safety line as the young man descended.

The rope ladder was not easy to negotiate, swinging left and right with each step, and it made him glad of the rope about his upper chest. It was a slow descent and by the time Nathan stepped on to solid ground almost fifteen minutes had passed and his body was bathed in sweat. Caleb's lasso was not quite long enough and Nathan had to slip out of it and complete the last seven or eight rungs without it, but the rope ladder had held.

'I'm down,' he yelled back up the shaft. 'Reckon Miss Ellie an' Miss Rachel should manage the climb down, but the little 'uns will need to be lowered.'

So began the slow, laborious task of getting them all down the shaft. By the time Caleb joined them almost an hour had passed.

'I sure ain't built for rope ladders,' Caleb gasped with a rueful grin.

A tunnel led away from the shaft. From it the sound of water was louder and the light brighter, so much so that Caleb doused the torch before they proceeded into the tunnel. The tunnel was a lot smaller in height and width than the mine tunnel and by the time they reached the end, Caleb and Nathan were bent double.

They eventually emerged on to a wide ledge that ran the length of a huge, dome-roofed cavern. At one end a curtain of water fell from a point some thirty feet up, cascading down to form a deep, foaming river that raced past them to disappear into an opening at the other end. At its highest point the domed roof was at least sixty feet above their heads and from waterfall to opening measured a length of 200 feet, while the distance from bank to bank was thirty feet. The racing water filled the cavern with a deep, hissing rumble.

They gaped in awe at the spectacle the cavern presented; even Caleb was affected by it. The light that filled the cavern came from a series of three openings high in the wall on the other side of the river in the form of silver beams that left the far ends in twilight shadow.

Caleb blew out his lips. 'Seen me some sights afore, but if'n this don' beat all,' he declared. He eyed the water. 'Don' know 'bout you folks, but I got me a thirst that could near empty that river.' A chorus of agreement followed his words. At this point the racing river was a good two feet below the ledge so they moved towards the waterfall until the ledge dipped and the surface of the water was only inches away. Here they dropped to their knees and dipped cupped hands into the cool, almost icy water and drank until their bodies could take no more. Afterwards, thirst slaked, they sat, backs to the rock wall and rested.

It was Rachel who saw the circle of dim light on the far side close to the waterfall.

'If'n that's the way out, how do we get to it?' Nathan spoke up, surveying the fast-flowing river.

'There's gotta be a way,' Caleb said, eyeing the river in both directions and finding no obvious way to get across. A short while later the way was found, a narrow, slippery path that led behind the waterfall. Here the rock wall shelved inwards to allow them to pass behind the cascade and not through it.

Caleb eyed the narrow path thoughtfully. It angled away from the wall towards the river. It shone blackly from a continual soaking of flying spray.

'Keep close to the wall an' move slowly,' he said as he led off. 'We don' want no one slipping an' falling in.'

All was going well, then disaster struck. They had completed half the journey to the other side when Molly, the youngest of the Baker girls, slipped and with a terrified scream disappeared through the tumbling curtain of water into the foaming river beyond.

9

For an instant there were just shocked, frozen faces, then the girls began to scream and call Molly's name. Caleb had to grab Rachel to prevent her from jumping in after her sister.

'It's no use. The current's too strong,' he yelled as she struggled in his arms, sobbing and calling Molly's name.

All eyes were on Caleb and Rachel so that none saw Nathan throw down his rifle and bandolier and shuck his jacket.

'I'll get her,' he yelled and before anyone could say anything he launched himself through the waterfall into the raging river beyond. Just before he hit the water he heard Ellie scream out his name, then the water took him in a powerful grip and dragged him forward, tumbling his body over until he eventually managed some sort of control.

The fast flow of the water dragged him along at what seemed breakneck speed towards the black hole into which the water disappeared. He had misjudged the speed of the water and at the rate it was carrying him along the journey from the waterfall to the hole would take a lot less than a minute. Molly must surely have been carried to her death. Her frail arms and legs would be no match against the flow of the river.

All around him the water boiled whitely over half-submerged rocks. He felt the toes of his boots scrape along the bottom and his knees and elbows rammed painfully against hidden rocks before the water deepened. The noise of the rushing water hissed loudly in his ears.

He looked ahead at the fast approaching tunnel-mouth, then he saw her. She had somehow managed to wrap her arms about the bark-stripped trunk of a tree that had been carried into the cavern and become wedged across the tunnel mouth.

Nathan steered himself towards her, using his feet to drag along the bottom in an attempt to slow himself. It seemed to be working until suddenly, ten feet from the hissing, roaring tunnel-mouth, the bottom fell away beneath him and the racing current carried him forward.

He slammed against the trunk with his upper chest and threw his arms over it as his feet and lower body were carried forward. Spitting water he inched his way along the trunk towards her.

'Molly, I'm coming. Hold on, girl,' he yelled above the noise of the water. She must have heard him for she turned her face towards him.

Nathan inched his way towards her until he was able to free one arm, wrap it around her waist and drag her to him. Her arms went around his neck and he held her tight. He fought the current with his feet, drawing his legs back. The coldness of the water numbed his body and he felt exhausted.

'It's all right, Molly. I've got you,' he

crooned. He could feel her body trembling against his.

'Nathan, hold on, boy!' Caleb's voice reached his ears above the roar and hiss of the water. Nathan turned his head. Caleb and the girls stood not twenty feet away on the opposite bank of the river, but that twenty feet could have been twenty miles. His arm around the trunk was weakening fast and he wondered how much longer he could hold on against the powerful pull of the current. He managed a weak smile.

'She's OK!' he yelled.

'Grandpa, what are we gonna do?' Ellie asked fearfully.

'Haul the boy in,' Caleb replied, removing the lasso from his shoulder. He had carefully kept it coiled after each time that it had been used and now he shook the coils out. He could see that Nathan was pretty much spent. Now it was down to him. 'Catch the rope, boy, an' tie yoursel' off an' we'll haul you in,' he bellowed. Nathan nodded to show he had heard.

'Hold tight to me, Molly. I'm gonna have to let you go for a while,' Nathan said to her and he felt her grip around his neck tighten.

Caleb opened the noose end of the rope, spun it over his head and let fly. It took two attempts before Nathan caught it.

'The water's running awful fast, Grandpa,' Ellie said nervously.

'That's why I'm gonna need you girls on the end o' the rope. Ain't gonna get but one chance at this so when I shout 'haul' you girls give it all you've got. Reckon 'tween us we'll beat this ol' river yet.' He eyed the two of them.

Ellie nodded. 'We'll beat it, Grandpa.'

'Yes, sir,' Rachel agreed and Katie and Sally nodded nervously.

By now Nathan had slipped the noose end of the rope around his neck and under his free arm. He held her tightly again.

'Listen up, Molly, we'uns are gonna take to the water agin. Mr Jones is gonna haul us in like fish on a line.

Now you hold on to me real tight an' I'll hold on to you. When I say, you take a big breath an' hold it as long as you can an' it ain't gonna be two shakes afore we're wi' the others an' safe. OK?'

She lifted her head and looked at him. 'You won't let go, Nathan?'

'I won't let go, button. You gotta trust me an' we 'uns gotta trust Mr Jones.'

She nodded and buried her head in his shoulder, arms tightening around his neck. He looked across at Caleb and the girls.

'Reckon we're 'bout ready, Caleb,' he shouted.

'Then what you waiting for?' Caleb hollered back.

'Take that breath now, button an' hold on. Ready?' He heard her suck in air and felt her head nod against the side of his face. With heart racing, Nathan sucked in air and released his hold on the log, transferring his hand to the rope as he felt himself being dragged into the tunnel.

'Haul!' Caleb yelled to the two girls,

at the same time leaning back and starting to pull, hand over hand.

The drag of the water made him suck air as he began hauling the two in against the racing current of the water. For an instant panic gripped Nathan as the roaring darkness closed around him, then he felt himself being pulled clear of the tunnel-mouth. Nathan twisted on to his back so that Molly was on top of him, her face clear of the water. He kicked his feet to try and help, but it was all down to Caleb and the girls.

Slowly, bit by bit, the two were hauled towards the bank. Sweat stood out on Caleb's face as his muscles strained and heaved. At last the relentless surge of the water lessened around Nathan. He felt himself being dragged along the rock face, away from the dreadful tunnel, and the water became shallower. Rocks and boulders scraped against his back and legs. He twisted over and drew his knees up as far as he could. They touched the bottom.

'Stop pulling,' he yelled. 'Reckon I

can stand now.' As the rope went slack Nathan settled back on his haunches and, still gripping Molly, rose shakily to his feet and staggered the last few feet to the bank. He handed Molly up to Ellie and Rachel before hauling himself up on to the bank. He sprawled at Caleb's feet, then rolled on to his back, sucking air into his aching lungs.

'Can you stand, boy?' Caleb asked.

'Reckon, sir,' Nathan replied. He pushed himself up on to his elbows and looked beyond Caleb to where Ellie and Rachel were tending Molly. 'How is she?' he called out.

'She's gonna be fine,' Ellie responded, rising to her feet to leave Rachel and Sally along with Katie to fuss over Molly.

Caleb helped Nathan to his feet, freed the young man from the rope, then recoiled it.

Ellie moved to Nathan's side and threw her arms about him.

'I thought I'd lost you for sure,' she murmured.

'Dammit, boy, if'n that weren't 'bout the stupidest thing I've seen in a long time,' Caleb said, slipping the wet, coiled rope over one shoulder and across his body.

'Grandpa!' Ellie flared up, stung by his words.

Caleb stared at Nathan, then a smile filled his face.

'But I'm real proud o' you, boy, real proud.' He stepped forward and gave a surprised Nathan a hug that almost had the young man's ribs cracking. Then he stepped back and eyed Ellie. 'You gotta fine man there, Ellie. You keep a hold o' him.'

'I intend to, Grandpa,' Ellie responded. She moved back to Nathan's side and slipped an arm about his waist, heedless of his wetness that soaked into her own dress.

'Need to get you warmed up, boy, an' them clothes dried out.' A wicked smile crossed his face. 'Reckon Ellie could think o' a way or two o' warming a man up.'

'Grandpa!' Ellie's voice was thick with embarrasment and a red flush filled her face. Even so she couldn't help looking up into Nathan's equally embarrassed face and giving a coy smile.

'Mind you,' Caleb went on relentlessly, 'cain't be doing that here. Young 'uns about.' He gave Ellie a wink and with a chuckle turned on his heels and headed back down the cave towards the lighted tunnel that offered a promise of escape from their underground world. 'Let's see if'n we cain't find the way out.'

★ ★ ★

They stood on the lip of a huge cave. Above them the cliff rose sheer to the sky and on either side it stretched away on a north-south line. Before them a steep scree slope flowed down into a tangle of gullies and low hillocks peppered with clumps of stunted, withered scrub. This in turn stretched away from the ridge in a series of tortured ripples that folded and creased the land for perhaps a mile before merging into the yellow sands of the Desierto de Altar that spread like some vast, frozen, yellow sea to the western horizon where the sun hung low in the sky.

Heat rose from the desert, flowing over them in a warm caress, but it was a deceptive heat. Caleb knew that as soon as the sun disappeared the warmth would give place to a shivering cold.

'We'll rest here for the night,' Caleb said. 'Get a fire going an' move out at first light.'

'Move out to where?' Ellie asked.

'Head north, mebbe find a place to get up on the ridge. Now, folks, we need to gather some o' this brush to build a fire. May as well get cosy for the night.'

Later, while the girls busied themselves making the fire, Nathan drew Caleb aside.

'You think we can beat the desert, Caleb?'

'Hell, boy. We've beaten everything else so far. Gotta believe we'll make it.' Caleb gave a shrug. ''Sides,' Caleb's face darkened, 'got me a burning need to meet up wi' a fella by the name o' Rafael Aguilar. Got me some unfinished business wi' that *hombre*.'

They spent the night huddled together in the cave, the fire keeping the desert cold out. They slept fitfully, each waking on and off. Caleb, during his periods of wakefulness, kept the fire going until, just before dawn, the scrub they had collected ran out.

Nathan awoke shivering as the first light of dawn greyed the entrance to the cave. The fire was now just a pile of barely warm ashes. He saw the figure of Caleb outlined in the entrance, staring out at the approaching new day. Nathan rose carefully so as not to waken Ellie and joined Caleb. All the girls appeared to have dropped into a deep slumber.

'Mornin', boy,' Caleb greeted softly.

'Caleb,' Nathan acknowledged, shoulders hunched, arms folded across his chest, hands rubbing the cold from his shoulders and upper arms. 'How far is it to Border Town, do you reckon?'

Caleb shrugged. 'Fifty mile. Could be more if'n we cain't find a way to get up on the ridge.'

'Gonna be hard walking for the girls.'

'Hard for us all, but we got one thing in our favour. The sun comes up on the other side o' the ridge so it won't be until midday that it'll shine on us. We can cover a whole heap o' ground afore then.'

'Then what?'

'Dammit, boy, you ask too many fool questions,' Caleb exploded. 'I ain't got no answer for you. If'n you're a churchgoing man you pray to the Lord for help. If'n you're a gambler you trust to luck.'

'What are you, Caleb?'

'A survivor, boy, just a survivor,' Caleb returned. 'Best get the girls up. It's time to move.' Before moving out Caleb spoke to the girls. 'I know you are all cold an' hungry. The cold won't last long but the hunger will. I cain't do a thing 'bout that, but I aim to get us to civilization. We got some water an' that'll have to be enough. We head north, follow the ridge. Come the time the sun clears the ridge we find a place to rest an' shelter out o' the heat. Later we'll probably get a coupla hours to cover some more ground afore night-fall. Jus' gotta keep in mind that every step we takes gets us closer to civilization. Let's hit the trail.'

In a ragged line, with Caleb leading and Nathan bringing up the rear, they left the safety of the cave and headed north in the chill dawn light.

As the morning lengthened the chill dissipated and was replaced by warm, dehydrating air. Even though the sun was hidden from them by the ridge they could watch its approach. A thin band of shining yellow stretched itself along the western horizon. The morning wore on and the band grew wider as the sun rose in the sky, the shadow cast by the ridge shortening.

It was a slow, torturous process, dipping into blind, brush-choked gullies that ended in a climb to sun-blasted hillocks before descending once again. It was hard going for the girls. The hems of their dresses continually snagged on the scrub, the material ripping as they dragged it free. At first they had carefully unhooked the material but as the morning wore on and the heat built they no longer took the trouble.

Katie and Molly suffered the most, being the youngest and smallest, until in the end they had to be carried, Katie on Caleb's shoulders and Molly on Nathan's. By the time the sun cleared the ridge Caleb estimated that they had probably covered less than five miles of ground.

The pace was too slow. They had used half the canteen of water already. At this rate it would be gone by the end of the day. What of tomorrow and the next day? Without water the picture was bleak. He could see the suffering on the faces of the older girls but they carried on without complaint.

They reached a point where the rippled effect of the land ceased temporarily and the sand swept to the base of the cliff like the sea coming into a bay. Half a mile ahead the gullies and hillocks started again and so far he had seen no break in the high, sheer rock face.

Caleb came to a halt and waited for the others to catch him up. He set Katie down on her feet and eased the ache from his shoulders while his eyes roved around.

'When we reach the rocks yonder we'll find a place to hole up an' rest.' They nodded. In just a few short hours the girls' faces had become drawn, their lips beginning to crack, but there was nothing he could do to ease their pain. 'C'mon, button, you can hold my hand,' he grunted to Katie before moving off again.

The sand undulated like a frozen sea in troughs and peaks, sucking at their feet as they stumbled on until Caleb jerked to a halt. He thought he had heard the jingle of harness and the whicker of a horse. Surely that couldn't be so, but the others had heard it too.

'Did you hear that, Caleb?' Nathan moved to Caleb's side.

'Thought I heard something,' Caleb admitted rubbing sweat from his eyes and peering west, unslinging the shotgun from his shoulder as a line of riders topped the dune ahead less than thirty feet from them. Caleb's jaw sagged in disbelief.

'Welcome, Señor Jones. I have been waiting for you,' came a sardonic voice.

'Salazar!' The name hissed from Caleb's lips accompanied by the ratchet-clicking of bullets being levered into breeches as two more of Salazar's men, on foot, appeared either side of them. Their rifles were aimed from waist level, their swarthy faces grinned beneath their helmets. The riders before them had drawn their rifles. The group was surrounded.

10

Caleb tossed his shotgun down and raised his hands to chest level, palms turned out in a gesture of surrender. Behind him Nathan followed his example, dropping his rifle into the sand.

'A wise move, Señor Jones,' Salazar observed with a smirk. He sat easy, nonchalantly, in the saddle obviously enjoying the looks of disbelief on their faces. 'But there is no escape from Salazar.' The smile slipped from Salazar's face. 'You and your *compadre* have caused me much trouble, *señor*.' He stared pointedly at Caleb. 'You will pay for that trouble,' he hissed.

'Our pleasure,' Caleb responded drily. He dropped his hands and stuck the thumbs of each behind the buckle of his gunbelt. 'How did you find us?'

The harsh look fled from Salazar's

face to be replaced by a laugh.

'You were never lost, Señor Jones. The moment you entered the mine your fate was sealed. It just required a little push on my part to make you enter.'

'You mean you wanted us to go in?'

'Precisely.'

'I don't get it, Salazar. Why? You could'a killed us all in the canyon.'

'A quick death? No, that would be too easy for you, Señor Jones. Instead I wanted to make you work for your inevitable death. Give you hope where, in reality, none existed. Let you get within touching distance of safety and then take it away.'

'You're all heart, Salazar,' Caleb replied mockingly. 'So I guess you knew there was another way out o' the mine?'

'It has been used as an escape route for *bandidos* many times. You are a resourceful man, *señor*. I knew that you would find the way out. Sealing up the entrance prevented you from waiting around until dark to try and make your escape by the way that you entered. Your every move was anticipated. I knew you would head north once you found your way out, for south would only take you deeper into Mexico. It was just a matter of waiting and here you are, as predicted. You are impressed, eh?'

'Very clever,' Caleb agreed. He became aware that Nathan had moved forward to stand at his side. He could admire the boy's courage, but this was the one time he could do without it. 'Get back behind me, boy,' he snapped.

'I'd appreciate to stand at your side, sir,' Nathan countered.

'Do as I say,' Caleb thundered harshly, staring hard at the young man.

Nathan stared back at Caleb, confused, then reluctantly stepped back.

Salazar clapped. 'Very gallant of you, señor. But who will they stand behind when you lie dead in the sand?'

Caleb casually eyed the two soldiers on either side before looking back at Salazar.

'You seem to have figured all the angles, Salazar.'

'Nothing has been left to chance. You and the boy will die. I will take the girls whom you fought so hard to save. The fort can be rebuilt, the men killed, replaced. All will be as it was before and everything you did will have been for nothing.'

Caleb pursed his lips. 'Sure looks that way, but then looks can be deceiving.'

'Are you expecting the cavalry to come riding to your rescue, Señor Jones?'

'Somethin' like that.'

Salazar laughed. 'How do you Americanos say? You will have to wait until hell freezes over?' Salazar laughed again. His words were translated for those who did not speak English and they too joined in the laughter.

Caleb glanced again to either side, then eyed Salazar, his own face breaking into a smile.

'Guess what, Salazar. It just froze,' Caleb yelled. What happened next was something Salazar could not have planned for, not even in his wildest dreams. Caleb went for his guns!

In a blur of fluid motion Caleb drew his weapons, thumbs pulling back the hammers as his arms lifted sideways in a move that in his heyday had given him almost legendary status; the ability to shoot at two separate targets in two different directions.

He did not even look as the guns in both outstretched arms erupted in unison and the two surprised soldiers cried out as bullets ripped into their bodies.

'Down!' Caleb roared as he threw himself down, did a complete sideways roll until he was on his stomach again, a yard from where he had been standing only seconds before. His arms now stretched out before him, the guns in his hands spoke again, firing at the line of soldiers on the dune ridge ahead. There was a ragged crackle of rifle fire from the soldiers as they shot at the spot where Caleb had stood only seconds before.

Two soldiers fell from their saddles. A

horse reared as a bullet creased its flanks, unseating its rider, its scream of pain unsettling the other horses. Caleb fired until his guns were empty. Another soldier went down, spraying blood, bone and brain matter from a hideous exit hole in the back of his head.

Nathan had dived for his rifle, at the same time grabbing up the shotgun and tossing it to Caleb before joining him. Salazar and his men had taken cover behind the dune.

Caleb came to his knees, reholstering one gun while he reloaded the other with shells from his belt.

'That was very impressive, Señor Jones,' Salazar's voice floated to them from behind the dune.

'Stick your head up, Salazar, an' I'll impress you some more,' Caleb shouted back, eyes raking the dune ahead for signs of movement as he deftly loaded the second gun, emptying his belt of spare bullets. He holstered his second gun before taking up the shotgun and shuffling backwards on his knees to where the girls lay. 'Make every shot count, boy,' he called to Nathan. 'We're gonna need all the shells we got an' then some to get us outta this.'

Now low on ammunition, no food and very little water, the outcome seemed inevitable. Even his prowess at impossible escapes had reached its limit. There was no escape this time; the others knew it but said nothing.

Nathan crawled across to them.

'That was mighty fine shooting, sir,' he said. 'Ain't seen the like o' it afore.'

Caleb gave a bleak smile. 'Kept me alive on a few occasions,' he said.

'What do you think they'll do, Grandpa?' Ellie asked nervously.

'Figure Salazar will have a few tricks up his sleeve,' Caleb replied grimly. 'We'll just have to keep our eyes peeled an' be ready.'

They did not have long to wait. Salazar had been quiet for some minutes now. It was Nathan who spotted a dark object arc into the sky from behind the dune. His sharp eyes caught a tail of smoke coming from it. He lifted the rifle to his shoulder and as the object began dropping he fired.

The dynamite bundle exploded in mid air, opening briefly into a red-petalled rose of fire that flared and was gone leaving a thin, grey smoke haze in its wake and an explosion that made their ears sing.

Figures appeared on the dune following the explosion expecting to see the group hurt or dead, only to be met by a hail of twelve-gauge buckshot from Caleb's shotgun, which dropped three more of Salazar's men.

'Nice shooting, boy,' Caleb called out to Nathan.

Two more of the dynamite bundles appeared in the sky. Nathan exploded one but the second one dropped on to the sand twenty feet from where they huddled. It exploded almost at once sending a fountain of sand into the air with a secondary spray flying outwards in all directions. The shock wave from the explosion pummelled their bodies.

Nathan was blown backwards, the rifle spinning from his hands as a wave of sand engulfed him.

Caleb threw himself flat, clutching his hat to his head as the wave of sand blasted over him. The sound of the explosion punched through his brain, leaving him feeling dizzy in its wake. He came to his knees as the rumble died away, aware that Salazar's men would follow the explosion.

Sand had got into his eyes, blurring his vision. Moving shapes like distorted shadows appeared before his tear-filled eyes. The shotgun spoke and a shadow fell with a cry of pain. Caleb dragged the back of a hand across his eyes in an attempt to clear his vision. It partially worked. He saw the butt of a rifle being thrust into his face, managed to deflect it with his forearms, but by now the shadows had solidified into grim-faced men surrounding him as he knelt in the sand.

A rifle butt was slammed between his shoulder blades, making him arch his back and tilt his head to the sky. His face twisted in pain as a searing, burning agony set fire to his spine and clawed at his ribs. The shotgun was knocked from his hands and he was hauled by noisy, yelling soldiers to his feet and prodded with rifle barrels until he dropped his gunbelt in the sand and raised his hands.

Salazar strode through the pall of settling dust to stand before Caleb, a smile wreathing his olive-hued features.

'You proved a worthy adversary, Señor Jones, but all to no avail. You and the boy will die and the *señoritas* will be mine.' By now a dazed Nathan had been dragged forward to stand with Caleb.

'You ain't won until I'm dead, Salazar,' Caleb grated.

'Then perhaps we should not keep you waiting, *señor*. Bring them!'

★ ★ ★

The rock rose from the sand like a jagged, broken tooth, the only feature

179

breaking the yellow monotony of the desert. Hands tied behind their backs, tethers about their throats, Caleb and Nathan had been forced to walk behind horses. The girls had been put astride saddleless horses, Ellie and Katie on one, Rachel, Sally and Molly the other. It was up to the girl in front to hold on to the horse's mane while the one behind held on to her. A tether around the horse's neck linked it to a rider who in turn led the string. Now, as the riders reined to a halt and Caleb and Nathan fell exhausted to their knees, the girls were allowed to dismount and huddled together in a frightened group.

Caleb and Nathan were hauled to their feet, a man at each arm. Salazar dismounted and approached the two, a smile on his scarred face. He peered at Caleb with his one good eye.

'Spreadeagle Rock. This is were you die, *señor*. The Indians once used it to tie down their enemies on and leave them to die and if the sun did not burn out their eyes first all they would see was the buzzards in the sky above waiting for them to die.' Salazar laughed.

'Pretty story,' Caleb croaked back from a dry throat.

Salazar gripped Caleb's jaw and squeezed, forcing his head up, making him look into his own dark countenance.

'Sometimes the birds do not wait for death,' he hissed. 'Sometimes they like to dine early while some life remains. The eyes, they like the eyes.' Salazar released his hold on Caleb and stepped back, grinning happily.

'You sure do have a great line in bedtime stories,' Caleb commented.

'Oh, it gets better. While you are praying for death you can think about your women and what is happening to them. Chico here' — a soldier who had moved to Salazar's side, grinned wolfishly — 'he favours the dark-haired *señorita*. Myself, the one with the hair of corn. The younger ones will work in the fort until it is their time . . . if they are lucky.'

'Dammit. You leave them alone,' Nathan shouted.

'Or you will do what, gringo?' Salazar taunted, staring at the anger-infused face of Nathan. 'You desire one yourself, eh!' It was a statement rather than a question. 'You should have taken her when you had the chance.'

Nathan let out a roar. His big arms shot up in the air as a fierce rage consumed him, breaking the grip of the two who held him. Two more soldiers rushed forward and Nathan's fists flew out, striking one with a jaw-snapping crack, poleaxing him to the sand. The other soldier threw himself at Nathan and both went down. All eyes were on the two as more men rushed to help their comrade.

Caleb felt the grip on his arms slacken as his two guards craned their necks to see what was happening. Caleb lifted his right foot and ground his heel into the instep of the man on his right. He heard bone crack in the boot. The man let out a high-pitched scream, released his grip and staggered aside, falling as his injured foot refused to support him.

The other guard turned his head as Caleb swung his right fist across his body and rammed it into the man's face, splitting his nose in a crunching strike that sent the man howling to his knees. Caleb threw himself at Salazar, but the one called Chico intervened with a punch to the stomach that sent Caleb to the sand. As he tried to rise a soldier stepped forward and drove the butt of his rifle into the base of Caleb's spine, forcing a cry from his lips as he arched his back. Caleb was temporarily paralysed by the agonizing pain that flared the length of his spine. Nathan lay semi-conscious on the sand, blood covering his face. Their bid for freedom was over.

Salazar gave a slow handclap.

'Bravo, *señores*. You are both very entertaining. Bring rope,' he called to a soldier. In a matter of minutes both men had their hands bound behind their backs, then they were forced to their knees and the same rope that bound their wrists was turned around their ankles and tied off, making it impossible for them to move.

'Your deaths will come later,' Salazar said gloatingly to Caleb. 'And for your own foolish actions,' Salazar's eye fell upon the cowering girls flicking from one to the other before settling on Molly, 'Chico will cut the throat of the small, dark-haired one. Bring her!'

Molly screamed as a soldier grabbed her arm and dragged her away. Rachel tried to stop him but received a rifle butt in the stomach for her trouble.

Molly was dumped unceremoniously at Salazar's feet.

Caleb stared at the man in horror.

'For God's sake, Salazar. She's just a child.'

'She pays for your mistake, Señor Jones, You attacked me and killed my men.'

'Give me a gun an' face me like a man, Salazar. Or mebbe there are no men in Mexico, just scum like you,' Caleb goaded, but Salazar just laughed.

'The thought is most tempting, but I would not like you to die quickly. Chico, the girl.'

Chico grinned, bent and hauled Molly to her feet by her hair, causing the youngster to scream out in pain. Holding her up by her hair, her feet barely touching the sand, Chico drew a knife.

'No!' Rachel screamed out. She tried to run forward but Ellie and Sally grabbed her. 'I'll do anything you say. Please don't harm her,' she implored.

'Yes, you will,' Salazar agreed. 'Chico.'

Still grinning, Chico moved the knife towards Molly's throat.

A single shot rang out. A small hole appeared in the middle of Chico's forehead. A split second later the back of his head exploded outwards in a crimson spray and he was thrown backwards, releasing his grip on Molly's hair, dead before he hit the sand.

Salazar turned and his single eye widened in surprise.

11

Less than a hundred yards to the east a lone Indian lowered a smoking Spencer rifle and stared defiantly at the group of soldiers. His sudden, silent appearance froze the group for an instant before Salazar grabbed for his pistol and called his men into a defensive wall. Half of them dropped into a kneeling position in front of the other half, who remained standing. All had rifles raised to their shoulders, trained on the lone Indian, waiting for Salazar's orders.

The Indian made no move to dive for cover. He was a young brave. A white hairband held his blue-black hair in position, sun glinted on his burnished body, which was clad only in a bead-decorated breech cloth.

Salazar drew his gun, but stayed his hand as, on either side of the Indian, others began to rise from the sand

where they had crawled unseen, forming a half-circle. Their appearance
caused panic amongst Salazar's men.

Caleb eyed the burnished, expressionless faces of the Indians, with their
colourful headbands holding their long,
dark hair in place. The Indians, mostly
bare-chested, some wearing leather
breech cloths, others in hide pants, but
all holding rifles, seemed to be waiting
for something or someone.

Caleb heard a frightened whisper
from one of the soldiers.

'Comanche!'

Salazar silenced the man with a harsh
command.

The soldiers' agitation increased as
the half-circle began to grow into a
full circle that completely surrounded
them. Caleb estimated there were
upwards of a hundred warriors.

'Seems you gotta problem, Salazar,'
Caleb called out.

'Why are the Comanche attacking
Mexican soldiers?' Salazar called out,
ignoring Caleb.

'How 'bout cutting us loose an' giving us our guns back. Reckon you're gonna need all the fire-power you can muster,' Caleb continued, only to receive a gun barrel in the face as Salazar turned furiously on him. The blow opened the skin just above Caleb's left cheek.

Caleb shook his head. 'Guess that means no,' he said.

'Salazar!' The name thundered out and Salazar turned away from Caleb, seeking the source of the voice. He found himself facing a mounted rider who had joined the circle, a red shirt open over his big, muscular chest. Caleb recognized the rider even without the tell-tale shirt. 'It is time to die.'

Red Shirt! The Indian he had rescued from the fort.

'Colonel . . . ?' A soldier looked around at Salazar, fear in his eyes.

'I hear you, Red Shirt, but be warned. Harm us and you and your people will be hunted down and hanged. Women, children, every last one of the Comanche nation,' Salazar blustered.

For an answer Red Shirt raised his rifle above his head and gave a yipping cry. The circle of braves took up the cry and began to move in. They came fast.

'Fire!' Salazar screeched. The pistol bucked in his hand as he fired at Red Shirt. The big warrior did not flinch in an arrogant display of bravado.

Yelling and screaming, a wave of Indians came over the rock formation, leaping over the girls crouching at its base, running between Caleb and Nathan. Guns roared, cutting down Salazar's men in a battle that lasted less than a minute, until only Salazar remained standing, pistol empty, three Indians dead at his feet. The braves closed in on him and within seconds his hands were tied behind his back with a rawhide thong while two lance-carrying braves stood on either side of him.

Red Shirt rode forward and gave a guttural command. Two braves, drawing knives, raced towards Caleb and

Nathan. The girls screamed as the knives were raised, the blades flashing in the sunlight. Caleb's heart threatened to burst out of his chest. Then, instead of his throat being cut, the bonds that held him and Nathan were slashed. Caleb fell forward, but strong hands gripped him and he was helped to his feet. By now Red Shirt had slid from his mount and stood before Caleb.

'Red Shirt does not forget the man who saved his life and that of Moon Flower.' A brave ran forward and a leather waterskin was thrust into Caleb's hands.

Caleb took a couple of long gulps. Warm, brackish, but the water tasted like nectar to his parched throat. He passed it to Nathan.

'Same here, Red Shirt. Caleb Jones ain't forgetting the man who just saved his, an' that o' my girls.' The girls, supplied with water, had come forward and joined Caleb and Nathan.

'Is Moon Flower well, sir?' Ellie

spoke up and Red Shirt's fierce gaze fell on her.

'She told of the kindness you showed her in the prison of the one eye. I thank you.'

'We all helped each other,' Ellie replied.

'I'm a mite curious,' Caleb spoke up, 'on how you came to be here when you did?'

For the first time a grim smile tugged at Red Shirt's lips.

'As the one eye followed you, so he was followed by a scouting party led by my son, Howling Wolf.' At the mention of his name a young brave stepped forward and Caleb recognized him as the one who had shot Chico. 'He sent back information to me and my braves.'

'I'm obliged.' Caleb nodded at Howling Wolf, then looked back at Red Shirt. 'He's a fine son.'

At that moment the women of the tribe appeared, led by Moon Flower astride a liver-spotted palamino. The women carried bundles that turned out to be food: a bread made out of maize, and cooked meat wrapped in yucca leaves. It was a signal for everyone to eat and Caleb, the girls and Nathan ate ravenously. The meat looked suspiciously like rattlesnake to Caleb, but he said nothing, not wishing to spoil their appetites as the girls speculated that it was chicken pieces.

With bellies full and thirst slaked, Nathan raised the question of Salazar, who appeared to have been ignored. Bound and guarded by two braves, he had been given no food or water.

'What will happen with Salazar?'

Red Shirt eyed the youngster. 'He belongs to the Comanche people.'

Caleb, eyes on Nathan, could see that the youngster was about to say something else, so he jumped in quickly.

'That was mighty fine food, Red Shirt.' Caleb struggled to his feet. 'But I reckon it's time we moved on. Got me some business wi' a certain gent in Border Town that needs to be attended to. It's just a matter o' how we get there.'

'The horses of the soldiers are yours. They have been made ready with food and water and my son will take you to the pass that leads through the mountains. From there it is half the passing of the sun to where you seek.'

'Obliged, Red Shirt.'

By now all the braves had risen and closed in on the group; there was a feeling of great expectancy as though something was about to happen. Caleb looked at the others and their puzzled looks showed that they too could feel it. Red Shirt approached and stood before Caleb.

'You have shown yourself to be a great warrior and a friend of the Comanche. You shall become a blood brother to Red Shirt.' Red Shirt drew his knife, folded his left arm, clenched his fist close to his left shoulder, then drew the sharp blade across the back of his forearm. As blood swelled from the cut he handed the knife to Caleb. Caleb took the knife.

'It'll be a great honour,' Caleb

responded solemnly, folding his own arm up and drawing the blade across the taut skin. Blood flowed and the surrounding braves began to whoop and holler as the two men pressed their bloodied arms together in the form of an X.

Red Shirt twisted his arm, gripped Caleb's hand and pushed it to the sky turning his body until the two men stood side by side.

'Caleb Jones shall be welcome in any Comanche lodge. Brother to Red Shirt and the Comanche nation,' he roared out to a renewed fervour of whooping cries and dusky, smiling faces.

'You and your people will always be welcome at the lodge of Caleb Jones,' Caleb replied as he handed the knife back to Red Shirt.

Two Indian women came forward with water in a gourd to bathe the cuts and wrap a strip of cloth around each.

The girls had watched the whole process in jaw-dropping amazement. Now silence fell over the assembled

Indians as Howling Wolf stepped before Nathan and the whole process was repeated amid a second wave of whooping calls. Red Shirt gave some orders and braves appeared, leading the promised mounts.

Caleb was given Salazar's horse and with a cry of delight retrieved his gun rig, which hung from the saddle pommel. He strapped the double rig on.

'Howling Wolf will lead you to the pass. Go in peace, Caleb Jones.' Red Shirt turned abruptly on his heel and marched away. This acted as a signal to the rest of the Indians, and suddenly the group found themselves on their own.

'Jones. You can't leave me.' Salazar's voice broke over them.

Nathan looked across at Caleb.

'We cain't do nothing, Caleb,' he protested.

Caleb threw Howling Wolf a quick glance. The brave, astride his horse, waited for them to mount up. Caleb couldn't tell from the impassive face whether the Indian had heard Nathan's words, but he was taking no chances.

'This sure beats walking, boy,' he sang out loudly, then he grabbed Nathan's arm and spoke in a low, urgent voice. 'That's just what we do, boy. Now mount up an' look happy. don' wanna give our new-found friends cause to doubt us.'

'Yes, sir,' Nathan mumbled.

'You girls OK?' Caleb called out, releasing his grip of Nathan.

The girls were already up. Ellie and Katie on one horse. Rachel and Molly on another and Sally riding alone. They all chorused their assenting replies and by that time Nathan was ready and waiting. Caleb breathed a sigh of relief and swung himself into the saddle.

'Lead on, Howling Wolf,' he called out.

Almost three hours later, as shadows lengthened and the sun began its fall towards the western horizon, Howling Wolf brought his mount to a halt and pointed. They had been following the ridge northwards and Caleb's keen eyes picked out the split in the rock wall that Howling Wolf pointed at.

'That will take you to the white man's town, Caleb Jones.'

Caleb nodded at the brave. 'I'm beholden to you, Howling Wolf.'

'I must return to my people.'

'Go in peace.' Caleb folded his right arm across his chest and banged his fist against his left shoulder in an Indian salute. Howling Wolf repeated the gesture.

'Take care, Howling Wolf,' Nathan called out, one arm across his chest.

Howling Wolf nodded at Nathan, smiled, wheeled his horse and rode back the way he had come.

The trail up through the pass was steep and at times they had to dismount and lead their horses, consequently night was almost upon them when they crested the trail and Caleb called a halt. They had the food the Indians had given them and, after rooting about in the saddle-bags of the horses, they found coffee, a pot, some battered tin mugs and lucifers. In no time Caleb had a small fire going and while they ate he set the coffee pot in the fire to heat up.

During the meal Nathan had been moodily silent while the girls had been excitedly chattering, relieved that their ordeal was over. Ellie had tried to draw Nathan out of the mood that gripped him, but with no success. Now, seated with his back to a rock, Caleb eyed the young man as he leisurely loaded bullets into a pistol he had found in the saddle-bag of the horse he had ridden.

'Ain't no good keeping it to yoursel', boy. Makes you bad company.' Caleb knew what was chewing at Nathan, but preferred the young man to spit it out.

Nathan's head snapped around. He sat before the fire, hugging drawn-up knees.

'It don' set right wi' me that we left Salazar wi' those . . . those . . . '

'Savages,' Caleb said. 'Guess they are

to our way o' thinking'. He nodded. 'But if'n it wasn't for them we wouldn't be here now.' The pistol loaded, he reached for his mug of coffee.

'For that I'm mighty grateful, but Salazar should have been handed over to the authorities — '

'Whoa there, boy,' Caleb cut in. 'A bunch o' gringos an' a tribe o' Comanche handing a Mexican army officer over to Mexican authorities for trial? You seem to be forgetting. We blew up a Mexican fort, killed half the soldiers there. More'n likely they'd hang us an' make Salazar a general.' Caleb took a mouthful of coffee and pulled a face. 'Damn me, what in tarnation do they put in this coffee?'

Nathan pulled a face. 'Put that way, I guess you're right, but — '

'Ain't no buts, boy. You saw what Salazar did to the braves back at the fort. You know what he had in store for us an' what he intended for the girls. He was a man in charge o' an army o' misfits. Men too bad for the regular army. The only way he could control them was to be worse than them.'

'Reckon more Comanche than we know of suffered at his hands; now it's their turn to pay back the man who caused them so much hurt an' misery.'

'But they'll torture him,' Nathan pointed out.

'Guess so, but it's their land, their law, their ways an' I for one ain't gonna stand in their way. I understand what you're saying an' that's good, but there are times when you have to turn away an' this is one o' them times.'

Ellie, who had moved to Nathan's side now spoke up.

'Grandpa's right, Nathan.'

Nathan looked at her and his face softened.

'Guess so,' he admitted reluctantly.

'Well, I'm glad that's agreed. Time to get some sleep,' Caleb spoke up. 'You'll be taking second watch, boy.'

'Watch?' Nathan looked puzzled.

'Don' forget we're still in Mexico, an' once news of what happened at the fort reaches Mexico City, we ain't gonna be too popular. I won't rest easy 'til we're back on American soil.' He held out the pistol to Ellie. 'Keep this wi' you, Ellie, we'uns have still a way to go.'

Ellie took the weapon with a solemn nod and slipped it into the apron pocket of her dress.

The following day, a little before noon, the group crested a ridge and below them, in the middle distance, Border Town sprawled like a wooden snake between Mexico and Arizona.

'Sure could do wi' a hot tub an' a new set o' clothes,' Nathan sang out and the girls chorused his wish. 'How 'bout you, Caleb?'

A grim, wintry smile played around Caleb's whiskered lips.

'Got me some business to take care o' first. Let's ride.'

12

Paco's was half-full. A dim, shadowy light came through the dirt-encrusted window and doorway. There were gaps between those who crowded the bar and only a few of the tables were occupied. It was a normal midday until a bundle of red dynamite sticks, a length of fuse spluttering and hissing angrily and throwing out sparks and acrid smoke sailed over the batwings, hit the floor and rolled towards the bar. Eyes turned in the direction of the dynamite and for a split second nothing happened. Then pandemonium broke loose.

Caleb had left Nathan and the girls at Jackson Small's saloon while he attended to his 'business'. Outside Paco's he waited.

Inside, everyone moved at the same time, rushing towards the batwings. Tables and chairs went over noisily.

Men shouted as they were shouldered aside in the rush to get to safety. Some in their panic tripped over the scattered chairs and went sprawling on the wooden floor only to find the boots of those still upright stamping painfully over them.

They spilled out through the batwings, tripping and falling over each other, their cries and yells causing those outside to stop and look in bewilderment as the stream of men tumbled and rolled on the rutted, hard-packed dirt of the wide main street.

Paco was the last out, only to find himself gripped by his shirt-front, swung around, his feet not touching the sidewalk, and slammed none too gently against the adobe wall. His eyes widened in astonishment and fear as he found himself staring into the grim, whiskered features of Caleb Jones.

'Going somewhere, *amigo*?' Caleb said.

'You!' The word hissed from Paco's lips and Caleb smiled.

'In person. Now where's Aguilar?'

'He is not here, *señor*.'

The smile left Caleb's face. 'Wrong answer.' With that he dragged and pushed Paco back through the batwings into the cantina. One chair was still standing. Caleb dumped the shaking man into it, removed the lasso that he was carrying over one shoulder and, before Paco realized it, the rope was coiled around his body and tied off, pinning the man in the chair.

Paco's eyes flickered to the fuse in the lethal bundle. The fuse was shorter now. His terrified eyes flashed back to Caleb's face.

'You are crazy. You will kill us both,' he screeched out.

'Reckon you could be right 'bout the crazy,' Caleb agreed mildly, 'but not 'bout the 'both' part. Another inch an' I'll be hightailing it outta here. Now where's Aguilar? Time's running out, Paco ... for you.' He cast an eye at the fuse. 'Reckon you got thirty seconds to answer afore I leave an' they scrape you off the walls. *Comprende, amigo?*'

Jackson Small sat at a table and viewed Caleb over steepled fingers.

'We meet again, Mr Chase. I thought you had left town.'

'I did, temporarily, an' I aim to make it more permanent when I've concluded a little business wi' a certain gent by the handle o' Aguilar.'

'Business, Mr Chase?'

Caleb shrugged. 'Nothin' that a bullet won't settle, only the *hombre* seems to have vanished an' I figured that, from one American to another, you might be able to point me in the right direction, so to speak. Man in your position gets to hear things.'

Jackson Small smiled and laid his hands flat on the table top.

'I take it that the explosion I heard a few minutes ago was your doing?'

Caleb shrugged. 'Paco couldn't answer my question.'

'Poor Paco,' Small said, but there was no sympathy in his voice.

'He's a cantina short, but I figured he was telling the truth so I let him live.'

'Very noble of you,' Small commented. 'What do you say, Rafael?'

'Very noble, Jackson.'

Caleb snapped his head up to the balcony above where Jackson Small sat to find himself looking into the grinning face of Rafael Aguilar. Aguilar was flanked on either side by four stone-faced Mexicans, their rifles trained on Caleb. Chairs scraped as the clientele of Small's Saloon beat a hasty retreat.

Caleb returned his gaze to Jackson Small. The men at the table with him had drawn their guns and were smirking over the barrels at Caleb. Even the barkeep had produced a shotgun.

'Hiram P. Chase, or should I say, Caleb Jones,' Small said. 'I'm afraid I cannot let you do your business with Rafael. Nothing personal, you understand, but here in Border Town an alliance exists that I cannot allow to be broken. Rafael controls one side of town and I, the other. We help each other and in that way peace exists between us. I'm sure you can appreciate that.'

Caleb, the initial shock over, shook his head.

'I must be getting old. I didn't see that coming.'

'You caused a lot of trouble, Señor Jones,' Aguilar called down. 'I only received news today of your eventful travels in Mexico. Mexico City is very angry. It seems you destroyed a fort and killed many soldiers. Colonel Salazar pursued you and your companions, but he and his men seem to have disappeared. Yet here you are. One would assume that Salazar failed in his mission.'

'Guess I'm just lucky,' Caleb returned.

'Unfortunately for you, your luck has just run out, Señor Jones. I do not intend to fail.' A smirk appeared on Aguilar's face but was wiped off by Caleb's reply.

'You did last time.'

Aguilar barked out an order in

Spanish and a man hurried away.

'You sure have been a busy person, Mr Jones,' Jackson Small drawled. Amusement danced in his eyes.

'Mebbe I ain't finished yet, Small,' Caleb snapped back, fixing his eyes on the saloon owner.

'I have heard you possess remarkable gun skills. Quite a legend in your day, so it seems, but that was then. Now is a different time and even the legendary guns of Caleb Jones will not save you. You are covered from the side, ahead and above. How would you like your headstone to read?'

'Grandpa!'

Caleb snapped his head up. Ellie and the other girls had been brought out and now stood at the rail on either side of Aguilar. It was Ellie who had called out to him. Nathan stood back from the rail, a man on either side, hands tied behind his back.

'I'm sorry, Caleb. Took us by surprise,' Nathan said.

'Ain't your fault, son. Reckon we

'uns are both surprised.'

'It was kind of you to bring the *señoritas* back, Señor Jones. Now I can sell them again. Much profit, eh? I have buyers ready and waiting and it will make our *compadre* in Desert Bluffs very happy.'

Caleb kept his emotions under control.

'You telling me that some *hombre* in Desert Bluffs is on your payroll?'

Aguilar's smile broadened. 'No, Señor Jones, we are on his,' came the surprising reply. 'Without his information we would not know where or when to strike.'

'an' who might this gent be?' Caleb grated out.

'You will die wondering, Señor Jones,' Aguilar taunted.

Caleb thought desperately. He needed a diversion, just a split second and mebbe, just mebbe . . .

'Nothing to say, Jones?' Small spoke up. 'A prayer, a plea?'

An idea filled Caleb's brain. It was

crazy and a long shot but it was all he had.

'Reckon this fella was what my old pappy called a high-kicker.' His eyes flashed to Nathan for an instant before settling on Aguilar. 'Yessir, a high-kicker. One o' them gents out to make money any way he can an' ain't too worried who he kicks to the ground in the process.' Again his eyes flashed to Nathan and adrenalin pumped as Nathan gave a slight nod.

'Very interesting, I'm sure,' Small said, sounding bored. 'I think it's time to die, Jones. With all my customers departed, I'm losing money.'

Caleb's eyes flashed to the people on the upper balcony, raking along them before settling on Nathan. He nodded and looked down towards Jackson Small.

'I can see that,' he agreed.

On the balcony Nathan tensed himself. The guards on either side of him were not holding him. He eyed the turned back of the man ahead of him, licked his lips, prayed he understood what Caleb was trying to say and taking all his weight and balance on his left foot he kicked out as hard as he could at the man by the rail.

The effect was impressive. The man cried out as the booted foot rammed like a mule-kick in the small of his back and thrust him hard against the rail. With an explosive crack the rail broke under the man's sudden weight and the man dropped on to the two gunmen to the right of Jackson Small, sending them flying.

Caleb went for his guns, left hand swinging in the barkeep's direction, right hand straight ahead. Both guns barked at once. The barkeep took a shot to the heart that sent him crashing back against a shelf of bottles and the shotgun flying from his grip. He twisted around, clawing at the shelf. Bottles scattered in all directions as he fell out of sight.

As the barkeep hit the shelf Caleb's deadly guns took out the two gunmen to the right of Jackson Small. Jackson Small himself had come to his feet and was clawing at his gun. It was free of the holster and swinging up to cover Caleb when two bullets caught him. One in the chest, the other in the forehead, blowing the back of his head out and spraying the wall behind him red.

Caleb threw himself sideways, hitting the floor and rolling. He collided with a table and sent it over as a hail of bullets came from the balcony above. He fired twice, narrowly missing Aguilar but hitting a man to the right. The Mexican flew backwards, his gun tumbling from his hand. The girls moved fast to get out of the falling man's way.

Nathan was on his back on the floor as Aguilar screamed out an order to the two Mexicans guarding Nathan. Both men had dropped to a crouch, dazed at what had happened. One rose to move forward. Nathan swung a leg, tripping the man who fell forward. A short section of broken rail thrusting up went through his throat, emerging red-stained through the back of his neck. The man squirmed and gurgled, tried to push himself away from the skewering stake when a bullet from Caleb's guns took him in the face and ended his agony in a shower of blood, bone-fragments and gobbets of grey brain matter.

On the balcony only Aguilar and one other remained alive. Aguilar rolled away from the balcony rail to the rear wall and twisted himself into a seated position, his back to the wall. From here he was shielded from below and could cover the top of the stairs that Jones would have to climb to get to him. Rage and fear vied for control of his face. His eyes settled on Nathan, who had struggled on to his knees.

'Now is your turn to die, gringo. Do you hear that, Jones? The boy will die an' then the *señoritas*. You cannot save them.' He levelled the gun at Nathan. The young man froze and steeled himself for the bullet that would end his life, but the shot that came was not from Aguilar's gun. It was louder, harsher and came from below.

The floor between Aguilar's knees exploded upwards. Aguilar screamed. Thick splinters of wood were driven deep into the backs of his knees and lower legs and pellets of heavy-gauge shot ripped up through the flesh as, below the balcony, Caleb, using the barkeep's shotgun, fired up through the boards. He had seen Aguilar roll away from the rail. Through the gaps in the boards he had judged his position.

Somehow, Aguilar pushed himself upright against the wall. With feet straddling the six-inch hole he fired his Colt through the hole until the hammer fell on empty chambers. Sweat poured from his agony-twisted face as the pain in his legs increased. From the knees downward the legs of his pants were stained red and in places the splinters of wood jutted through the flesh. He threw the useless gun aside and drew a second from inside his coat, ready to continue firing.

'Time to die, Aguilar.' The flat, emotionless words caused Aguilar to freeze, then snap his head up and to the right. Through eyes filled with pain-tears he saw the blurry form of Caleb on the balcony at the head of the stairs. In one hand Caleb held the shotgun, in the other a pistol taken from one of Small's gunmen. Caleb's own guns, empty, had been returned to their holsters.

Aguilar ran a shaking hand across his eyes to clear his vision.

'It comes to us all, *señor*,' Aguilar hissed and raised the pistol.

A bullet from Caleb's gun caught the Mexican mid-chest, spinning him along the wall until eventually he slid down into a splay-legged sitting position. The gun fell from his grasp as he clutched at the wound that would eventually end his life.

Caleb turned his eyes on the one remaining Mexican. He raised the shotgun in a single-handed grip.

'Do you want to die, *hombre*?' he barked.

Sergio Calvares dropped his gun and raised his hands above his head.

'No die, *señor*,' he said quickly in a shaking voice.

'Good. I'm tired o' killing. Get out o' here, move, vamoose.' Caleb waved the shotgun and Sergio was only too pleased to comply.

Caleb cut the ropes binding Nathan's wrists and pushed the shotgun into the young man's numb hands.

'Take care o' the girls,' Caleb grunted. He moved forward until he stood over the dying Aguilar.

'Time to clear your conscience, Aguilar. Who was the man in Desert Bluffs you worked for?'

Aguilar lifted his head. The grey pallor of death infused the olive skin of his face.

'I am dying, *señor*. Why should I give you his name?'

'For that reason. Small's dead an'

you will be soon, but this other *hombre*, he's gonna stay alive. Mebbe get himsel' another Small, another Aguilar an' carry on. That sure don' seem right. You do all the dirty work an' he lives. He'll forget all 'bout you an' mebbe live till he's an old man. You paid the ultimate price. Only seems fair he should pay as well.'

Below, in the bar-room behind the counter, a spreading pool of whiskey reached the smouldering stogie the barkeep had had in his mouth when Caleb's bullet smashed into his heart. With a dull crump the whiskey ignited with a blue flame.

Blood dribbled from Aguilar's lips and his eyes seemed to have difficulty focusing. He said something that Caleb did not quite hear. Caleb dropped to his knees beside Aguilar.

'Didn't quite catch that, *amigo*,' Caleb prompted and bent his ear close to the bloodied lips. Aguilar's lips moved again in a dying whisper, then his head lolled forward on his chest and his wheezy breathing ceased.

Caleb rose slowly to his feet, shaking his head, a shocked expression on his face. The name that Aguilar had whispered with his final, gasping breath had been the last one he would have thought of.

'Caleb! We're on fire!' Nathan's alarmed shout jerked Caleb back to the present. Behind the bar the blue flames had turned to an angry red as the dry boards of the floor ignited and sent clouds of black smoke into the air.

'Time to move,' Caleb roared and he led them down the stairs. They ran for the batwings and the open air beyond, chased by the ever-increasing, billowing smoke as the crackling flames climbed the wall behind the counter. 'FIRE!' he yelled at the people gathered outside, sending them into panic. If anyone harboured thoughts of trying to stop the fleeing group, that idea was forgotten. They reached their waiting horses without hindrance and rode off unnoticed.

* * *

The hoedown in the Desert Bluffs meeting hall was in full swing when the door opened and Caleb, followed by the girls and Nathan entered. They had had no chance of the much needed bath and fresh clothes. With the knowledge that the Mexican army was riding on Border Town looking for them, Caleb had felt that hightailing it out of town was the best course of action. Apart from taking food and water, they had left as they had arrived and as they now looked, as they entered the hall: dirt-streaked, clothes torn, hair matted.

There were shocked cries as they strode into the hall, people drawing back to allow them passage. The band stopped playing and Luke Jarvis, the deputy, stepped forward, a serious look on his thin face. He held up a hand.

'Hold up now folks — '

'No, you hold up, Luke Jarvis.' Ellie stepped forward, hands on hips. She saw Luke's eyes widen.

'Ellie, Ellie Taplow, is that you?'

'And it's me,' Katie pushed forward.

Around the hall whispers were going up.

'That's the Taplow girls.'

'Ain't that Nathan Burgess?'

'Katie?' Luke looked confused. 'But you girls was took.'

'An' woulda stayed took if'n it weren't for Grandpa an' Nathan.'

'Mr Jones.' People were beginning to close in around the group, eager for news. Luke looked back over his shoulder. 'Sheriff. It's Ellie an' Katie an' — '

'I can see who it is.' Walt Danvers came forward, watched closely by Caleb. 'So you made it after all, against all the odds.'

'You'd better believe it, Walt,' Caleb replied mildly. 'You got something here to lay the dust in a man's throat?'

'Only lemonade. Saloon's the place if'n you want something stronger.'

'Lemonade'll do fine. Reckon you

girls could do wi' some lemonade?' A chorus of yeses went up from the girls. 'By the way, these are the Baker girls. Reckon the deputy here'll get you some lemonade, ladies.'

'Be my pleasure. You all come along wi' me.'

'How'd you find them?' There was a tightness in the sheriff's voice.

'The hard way,' Caleb said, eyes fixed on the sheriff.

A small, portly man in a store-bought suit pushed himself forward.

'Mayor Fred Dakers, Mr Jones. I'd like to shake your hand, sir.' He held out a hand.

Caleb took it, saying, 'Sorry 'bout the dirt, Mayor. Been a while between baths.'

'I ain't afeared o' no dirt, Mr Jones. Proud to shake your hand, sir.' The mayor's face was wreathed in smiles. 'I own the general store. All you folks are welcome to come by an' pick up some new clothes an' it won't cost you a cent.'

'That's mighty kind o' you, Mayor,

an' happen you'll have to pick up a new sheriff at the same time.' Caleb dropped the mayor's hand and faced Walt Danvers. The sheriff's face had gone white.

'I don' understand, Mr Jones,' the mayor said.

'Seems Nathan an' I were on to a hiding to nothing the moment we entered Border Town. Someone tol' 'em we were coming an' who we were. Someone from this town.' Caleb raised his voice and a heavy silence filled the hall.

'You mean someone in this town was working for Aguilar?' There was outrage in the mayor's voice.

'On the contrary, Mayor, Aguilar was working for him. He supplied the information so that Aguilar knew just where an' when to strike. Ain't that right, Sheriff?'

'What do you mean?' Danvers looked uncomfortable.

'Why, afore he died Aguilar gave us the name o' the man in Desert Bluffs who ran the whole shooting match. Sheriff Walt Danvers!'

'That's a lie,' Danvers burst out.

'Why should a dying man tell a lie?' Caleb asked.

''Cause I chased him a few times. Damn near caught him one time,' Danvers shot back heatedly.

'I don' think so,' Caleb returned.

'You gonna believe a murdering scum like Aguilar over me, Fred, for God's sake?' The sheriff turned to the mayor.

'That's a mighty serious accusation, Mr Jones. Walt here's been sheriff o' Desert Bluffs for the past twenty years. The word of a dead man, 'specially one like Aguilar, ain't gonna mean much, 'less you got proof?'

'Proof, Caleb. You need proof,' Danvers said quickly.

'Could be a problem wi' Aguilar dead an' Jackson Small in a similar position,' Caleb admitted, nodding. 'Jackson Small, now he didn't say much afore he died. Fact o' the matter is that he didn't have the time, but unlike Aguilar ol'

Jackson was a careful man. So careful that he' — Caleb reached into a side pocket of his coat and drew out a small, red-covered book that he held aloft — 'kept a record o' when and where an' the money shared 'tween the three o' you. Guess he didn't wanna be cheated.' Caleb gave a chuckle. 'It's all here, dates, times. I reckon that's proof enough.'

A gun appeared in the sheriff's hand.

'Hand that book over, Jones.'

'Why'd you do it, Walt? Sheriff's pay not enough for you?'

'The book, Caleb.'

'Ain't nowhere to run, Walt,' Caleb said mildly.

'I got friends in Mexico. Once across the border I'll be safe. Luke, if'n you're thinking o' going for that hogleg you're toting, think agin. Now shuck the gunbelt or I'll put a bullet in the mayor.' As he finished talking to his deputy he swung the gun on the mayor. 'You too, Caleb.'

'That proof enough for you, Mayor?' Caleb asked.

'You folks stay back an' no one'll get hurt.'

'Do as he says,' Mayor Dakers shrilled. Then the shot rang out.

Walt Danvers jerked as a bullet punched a hole in his chest, a look of surprise on his face. He took a couple of unsteady steps before turning and facing his executioner.

All eyes had been focused with shocked disbelief on the sheriff, so no one had noticed Ellie take out the gun that Caleb had given her on the trail.

'You had my ma killed,' Ellie Taplow said, tears rolling down her cheeks. She held a gun in both hands, arms straight out before her. 'She was a good woman. She didn't deserve to end her life that way.' The gun roared again and a bullet burrowed deep into Walt Danvers's gut.

He sank to his knees, his gun falling from his hand, then he pitched forward and lay still.

Caleb darted to the distraught girl.

'It's over, Ellie.' He took the gun from her trembling hands. She turned her tear-stained face to him.

'I had to do it, Grandpa, for Ma's sake.' Her voice was small and lonely.

Caleb smiled at her. 'You did right, honey.' He held out his arms and she fell into them, sobbing softly as the other girls gathered around. After a few minutes Caleb motioned Nathan forward and turned Ellie into his arms.

'Justified, wouldn't you say, Mayor?' He raised an eyebrow as he turned and faced the shaken mayor.

'Totally,' the mayor replied as the colour slowly returned to his cheeks. 'The man admitted his guilt, thanks to that book.'

Caleb smiled. 'This,' he held up the book. 'It ain't nothing. I found it in the saddle-bag o' the horse I was riding.'

'You mean it didn't contain records of his dealings wi' Aguilar?'

Caleb casually tossd the book onto the dead body of Walt Danvers.

'It's empty, but then he didn't know that!'

We do hope that you have enjoyed reading this large print book.

Did you know that all of our titles are available for purchase?

We publish a wide range of high quality large print books including:
Romances, Mysteries, Classics
General Fiction
Non Fiction and Westerns

Special interest titles available in large print are:
The Little Oxford Dictionary
Music Book, Song Book
Hymn Book, Service Book

Also available from us courtesy of Oxford University Press:
Young Readers' Dictionary
(large print edition)
Young Readers' Thesaurus
(large print edition)

For further information or a free brochure, please contact us at:
Ulverscroft Large Print Books Ltd.,
The Green, Bradgate Road, Anstey,
Leicester, LE7 7FU, England.
Tel: (00 44) **0116 236 4325**
Fax: (00 44) **0116 234 0205**

They wanted to hang Giles Clanahan for a murder committed by Jake Shockley. To clear his name and bring Shockley to justice, Clanahan flees across the Arizona desert and stumbles across a plot. A band of ex-Confederate soldiers, led by Hammond Cole, plans to seize a valley known as Canoga and drive off the new settlers living there. The only man aware of the plot is Clanahan, and he must play out a bloody game on the open range.

THE AVENGERS OF SAN PEDRO

Edwin Derek

In Texas renegades attack San Pedro, a Mexican settlement, massacring its inhabitants. Brad Miller pursues them into New Mexico, but then a storm forces him to shelter in a ranch owned by Jane Latham. Jane is caught up in a feud between the Bar Zero ranch and the Blackwash silver mine. When a range war breaks out involving the renegades, can Brad, aided by a deadly gunman, bring justice to New Mexico, where the only law is the six-gun?

DIE THIS DAY

Dempsey Clay

When their troubled town was again without a peace officer to enforce the law, the citizens agreed on what must be done: forget the cost and hire a town-tamer. The famed marshal seemed to meet all their requirements — until the day gun hell erupted again. The town looked confidently to their hero to deal with the trouble — while only the marshal himself realized that this town — and this adversary — might prove the one to put him in his grave.

LANIGAN AND THE SILENT MOURNER

Ronald Martin Wade

Shawnee Lanigan is a half-breed man-hunter. He's commissioned by a grieving grandfather to track down Marsh Kennebec, who murdered the old man's daughter and her husband. However, Lanigan finds himself fighting for his life against outlaws and corrupt lawmen attempting to bar his path. He finds the killer but, outnumbered and outgunned, he's soon standing trial for his life before a jury of desperados. If convicted, he will hang. If found innocent, he faces a duel to the death.

BLAST TO OBLIVION

Chap O'Keefe

Fifteen years in a penitentiary had warped his mind, and Zach Skann came to Denver toting a deadly 12-gauge Greener shotgun . . . His victim, mines investor Ryan Bennett, had been responsible for his incarceration and his comrades' hangings. Subsequently, gun-for-hire Joshua Dillard was summoned by Bennett's sister Flora to seek the truth about her brother's murder. To clear up the accusations and trickery, Joshua rode to a mining-town hell-hole. There the trail of inquiry became a trail of more blood!